Entry Level

Entry Level

Stories by

Julie McIsaac

SEROTONIN | WAYSIDE

INSOMNIAC PRESS

Edited by Jon Paul Fiorentino

All rights reserved. No part of this publication may be reproduced, stored in a retrieval system or transmitted, in any form or by any means, without the prior written permission of the publisher or, in case of photocopying or other reprographic copying, a license from Access Copyright, 1 Yonge Street, Suite 1900, Toronto, Ontario, Canada, M5E 1E5.

Library and Archives Canada Cataloguing in Publication
McIsaac, Julie
    Entry level / Julie McIsaac.

Short stories.
ISBN 978-1-55483-068-8
Ebook ISBN 978-1-55483-081-7

I. Title.

PS8625.I82E68 2012   C813'.6   C2012-900784-6

The publisher gratefully acknowledges the support of the Canada Council, the Ontario Arts Council and the Department of Canadian Heritage through the Canada Book Fund.

Printed and bound in Canada

Insomniac Press, 520 Princess Ave.
London, Ontario, Canada, N6B 2B8
www.insomniacpress.com

Canada ▮◆▮

THE CANADA COUNCIL | LE CONSEIL DES ARTS
FOR THE ARTS | DU CANADA
SINCE 1957 | DEPUIS 1957

ONTARIO ARTS COUNCIL
CONSEIL DES ARTS DE L'ONTARIO

To Mae and Myrle

Contents

The Cashier

Because I was new, I did not work cash alone. I was paired up with a more senior member of staff. Debbie, who was training me, had been with the company for five weeks. She was an overweight woman with a perm.

The first thing Debbie did was point out to me that my name tag was upside down. Earlier that day, I'd been issued a red vest with a zebra embroidered on the back and a blue name tag that said KATHLEEN in crayon-style font. I had to supply my own white dress shirt, blue jeans, and black running shoes. This was tough to coordinate, since I was still living out of boxes.

I flipped my name tag around. My vest didn't fit, and I had to keep pulling it down to cover my stomach, which I was sure had gotten bigger since I'd moved back home. Debbie and I took checkout number four. I tried to log in to my register the way I had been shown, but it wasn't working. The till kept saying Invalid PLU/SKN Code.

"What's happening?" asked Debbie.

"I have no idea," I replied.

Debbie looked more closely at the register and flicked a piece of lint from the buttons with her pinky finger.

"You must have hit *total* instead of *enter*," Debbie said.

"No, I'm pretty sure I hit *enter*."

"No, you must have hit *total*." Debbie tried with her employee number and was able to log in. "See, I logged in just fine."

"Okay, I'll try it again," I said, and I got the same rejection: Invalid PLU/SKN Code.

"That's weird," said Debbie.

"Not really," I said. "That's exactly what happened last time."

"Well, try paging Jane or Barb."

I didn't know who Jane or Barb were. And was I to page them both and they decided who answered, or did I have to decide and page one or the other? And how did I page?

Debbie read the confusion on my face. "Have you ever paged anyone before?"

"No. Jason showed me how to yesterday, but I've never actually done it."

"Okay, I'll show you." Debbie picked up the phone at my till. "Dial 800, then listen for when the music in the store stops and there is a click, then say your page." Debbie did as she had said. I heard her fuzzy voice splice into a Christmas carol: "Jane, call two-two-four please. Jane, two-two-four." Then she hit the release button and hung up the phone. "Always make sure you hit the release button after every page before you hang up."

I remembered Jason telling me that. If you didn't hit the release button, the sound of the receiver being hung up would be paged over the whole store. It sounded awful.

While we waited for Jane to call back, Debbie played with one of her earrings and I bit my cuticles. She looked at me and opened her mouth to say something, but then the phone rang and she answered it.

"Kathleen can't get her login to work....

Yes, we tried that.... Okay.... No, my login works fine.... Okay, thanks."

Again, Debbie and I waited at register four.

"So," Debbie said. "Do you go to school?"

"No." I smiled. "I'm finished school."

"Oh." Debbie started playing with her earring again. I looked across the store to a crowd of shoppers and noticed a girl I'd gone to high school with. I hadn't seen Cynthia McLean since eleventh grade, when she'd gotten pregnant and dropped out. My mom and her mom had been friends too, but they'd lost touch. In high school, I'd always meant to give Cynthia a call and offer to babysit, since I liked kids when I was younger. My mom talked me out of it though. I hoped that Cynthia wouldn't notice me.

Then Jane arrived, breathing heavily as though she'd been running. She held a clipboard in one hand, and there was sweat forming around her hairline.

"What is the problem with Kathleen's login?" she asked.

"It's not working. Mine works fine though," Debbie said.

"Okay, well, just let her use your number for now—" Jane focused on Debbie's blue name tag. "—Debbie—and I'll make a note to look into it later." She scribbled on her clipboard. "I'll also note that she's using your number, in case there are any mistakes."

"Okay," Debbie said.

Jane left, and Debbie punched her number into my till.

I was ready to sell. Well, not really sell, more like tally.

My first two customers went smoothly. They both bought toys from the girls department. The first customer, an older man with lots of silver hair and a big silver mustache, bought a doll that cried when you shook it. The second customer, a middle-aged woman with a perm and a leopard-print winter coat, bought a giant Barbie head that you could put real makeup on. They both paid cash, and I politely thanked them for choosing Toys-O-Rama.

Debbie continued to remind me that she was there if I needed help.

"Are you offering people a gift receipt?" she asked.

"I forgot," I told her, which was no excuse, judging by the look on her face.

The next customer at my cash register was a middle-aged woman with lots of gold jewellery and the same hairdo as Debbie. A red-faced toddler squirmed in her shopping cart. Tears rolled down his cheeks while he yelled and flapped his arms.

"Happy Holidays. Thank you for shopping at Toys-O-Rama. Did you find everything okay?"

The woman did not answer but began piling her purchases on the tiny counter in front of her. I could not possibly scan and bag her items as rapidly as she hurled them at me, but I tried, moving so quickly that I almost forgot to offer a gift receipt. Almost.

"Would you like a gift receipt?"

She nodded.

And I began to scan and bag, scan and bag, scan and...I felt a slap on my shoulder. I turned to see Debbie, stretching over from the till in front of mine where she was helping another trainee, her belly pressed against the counter.

"Don't forget to ask her if she wants a gift

receipt," she said.

"I know," I said, focusing on the pile in front of me.

After paying for her purchases, the woman with the toddler carefully examined her bill.

"So, you see what you did!" She thrust the bill under my nose. "You double-scanned." She was right. I'd charged her twice for the same item.

"What did she do?" Debbie asked the woman, quickly returning to my register.

"She double-scanned an item." The woman shook the bill so hard that her gold bracelets jingled and her gold earrings swayed.

Debbie carefully looked over the receipt and saw that the woman was right.

"Okay, you need to page a manager," Debbie told me.

"Who do I page?" I asked.

"The manager on duty," Debbie replied.

"Who's that?"

"Look at the time sheet."

"What time sheet?"

"You didn't get a time sheet?"

"I don't know what a time sheet is."

"Is this going to take very long?" the woman asked. Her toddler moaned.

"Try paging Clarissa," Debbie suggested. I had encountered Clarissa earlier, in the break room. She looked about eighteen, and I had no idea that she was a manager. I had given her a quick smile, but because of her braces, she returned with more of a scowl.

I picked up the phone receiver, dialled, and waited for my cue. The music stopped, there was a beep, and then I said, "Clarissa, call two-two-four please. Clarissa, two-two-four." I hung up the phone without hitting the release button.

"Okay, there's no way she heard that." Debbie picked up the phone and did it again, this time talking very loud into the receiver. She pressed the release button and hung up the phone. "Also, don't forget to press the release button before you hang up."

"Sorry," I said.

"How long will it take for Clarissa to call back?" The woman tapped the counter as she waited. She did not look at her toddler. His face was covered in tears and mucus. He was likely as red and slimy as the day he was born.

"Shouldn't be too long at all." Debbie smiled.

The phone at my till rang and I answered it. It was Clarissa.

"I'm on my lunch," she said and then hung up. I wondered if the scowl from earlier had nothing to do with her braces. I looked at Debbie.

"Clarissa is on her lunch," I said.

Debbie grabbed a sheet of paper from beside my register. I assumed that this was the time sheet. She scanned over the long list of names while the woman sighed and gasped in disgust. The toddler sat crying in the shopping cart and stretched his chubby arms into a V above his head.

"Try calling Karen," Debbie suggested.

I paged Karen, this time making absolutely sure to hit the release button before hanging up. I saw Debbie huff and shake her head, though I couldn't figure out why.

The phone rang at my till and I answered quickly. "Hello?"

"You called me." It must have been Karen.

"Yeah, can you come to register four?"

"No, I'm in the baby department right now."

"Well, I'm having a hard time figuring out who the manager on duty is."

"Well," Karen said, "you need to find out who the manager on duty is. Oh, and next time you make a page, don't forget to press the release button before you hang up." She hung up.

I turned and stared at Debbie. "Karen is in the baby section."

"This is ridiculous!" the woman hollered. She threw her hands in the air and then let them slap down on the counter.

"Okay, try Barb."

I paged Barb, making sure to press the release button before hanging up.

Debbie looked at the woman. "Those are lovely earrings," she said.

"Thank you," said the woman as she pinched her lips together and gripped the receipt.

Barb phoned back and agreed to meet us at register four as soon as possible. In the meantime, Debbie continued to try and make small talk with the woman. I stared at the toddler. He had green eyes under all those tears.

Barb arrived and asked Debbie what the problem was without looking at me.

"Okay," said Barb to the woman. "Unfortunately, I need to return your entire purchase and then ring everything in again."

"What?" the woman yelled. "I can't wait that long."

"Well, that's the only way to do it," Barb explained.

"Oh my God!" said the woman. "Forget it!" She grabbed her items and threw them into her shopping cart. The toddler kept crying with his arms raised in a V as he was wheeled through the automatic doors. Barb, Debbie, and I remained crowded at register four.

Barb looked at me. "Try and be more careful next time. Oh, and when you page, make sure you press the release button before you hang up."

"I know. I've been told," I said. Barb walked away. I turned and saw Debbie still perched beside my register, awaiting my next mistake and her next opportunity to correct it. A customer wandered toward the checkout.

"Sir," Debbie called for his attention. "Can we help you over here?"

My shift ended, and I headed straight home. When I got there, my mom and dad were sitting at the kitchen table, playing cribbage, smoking cigarettes, and drinking. Mom had a light beer, while Dad preferred rum and Diet Coke.

"Want to play some cribbage?" Dad asked while grey smoke shot out his nostrils.

"I don't know how." I sat beside them at the table, with a plate of cold leftovers.

"You don't know how to play cribbage!" my mother bellowed. After most things my mother said, she would make a little noise, like a tiny grunt or a nervous humming sound. "I can't believe you could grow up in this house and not know how to play cribbage! Hmph."

"When I'm done eating, I'll play a hand," I said. My mother slid the ashtray away from where I was sitting, down to the other end of the table.

"Hey!" Dad shouted. "I can't reach it way over there!"

"Well, your daughter's eating," Mom said.

"Well, I can't reach it way over there!" Dad moved the ashtray back beside me. "That's better," he said.

"I think tonight's the night Ken Jennings loses," Mom said.

My parents were obsessed with Ken Jennings. He was beating the pants off of everyone on *Jeopardy!*, winning more than any other contestant in the history of the game show. Dad checked the Internet every day to see what the insiders had to say about Ken's winning streak. Apparently, everyone agreed that Ken would lose in his seventy-fifth game, which was tonight. According to Dad, even the producers of the show had supported that information, although I couldn't understand how he knew that for certain. My parents talked about Ken constantly to anyone who would listen.

"They say tonight's the night," my mother had said to someone on the phone last week. That was when Dad had thought Ken would lose originally, although he had apparently just read the date wrong or misunderstood something.

"What do you mean 'what night'?" Mom had continued over the phone. "You know, don't you watch *Jeopardy!*...? Yeah, well, Ken's been winning for a couple months now.... Yeah, well, I thought you'd of known that.... Well, tonight's the night he loses."

My mother didn't pursue a conversation about Ken Jennings with me.

"Did you send that email?" she asked me as I began to relax after my meal.

"What email?" I asked.

"The one I cut out of the paper for you? Hmph."

"What email did you cut out of the paper?"

"About the web designer?"

"Oh, right."

Mom was in the habit of cutting out articles from the newspaper that she thought I'd like. Often they were either personal interest stories about cats or news articles about how poorly Wal-Mart treated its staff. But lately she had taken to cutting from the classified section job descriptions she thought I might be interested in. Her latest finding was for a part-time web designer for a small marketing company located in Mississauga. I couldn't support myself part-time, had absolutely no experience in web design, was not interested in marketing, and hated Mississauga.

"No," I said. "I didn't email them."

"Why not? Hmph."

"Because I don't want to be a web designer," I said.

"You'd rather be a cashier?"

"I don't want to be a cashier. I just am one."

"Well," she said. "Then apply for the job doing web design. Hmph."

"Don't start about this."

"What am I starting? I'm not starting anything."

"Yes you are."

"All I did was ask you if you'd sent an email. Hmph."

"I'm going to my room." I went downstairs, leaving my dirty plate on the table.

"No," Mom said. "I didn't mean you had to leave."

"Well, I have no idea what you mean,

ever." I entered my room and closed the door. I could hear the TV blaring and my parents talking, about me, over it. This was all the peace and quiet I could hope for.

I was stuck in my room with its bare walls and empty bookshelves. I hadn't gotten a dresser yet, so all my clothes were in garbage bags on the floor. On my bed was a thin quilt that my grandmother had made for me when I was born. It was orange and yellow with a large cartoon duck in the centre. There were two thin pillows that made my neck hurt every morning.

I had a small nightstand, and I could see that my mom had left me some reading material. I glanced at the title on the small pamphlet: "Disgusting and Inhumane" was written in large red letters over a black and white photo of a fetus. Inside, a comic strip showed a cartoon fetus being removed from a cartoon womb by a pair of enormous cartoon hands. The accompanying text explained that the fetus could not be pulled out easily. Its head was too big and would get stuck inside the uterus. If a doctor tried to remove it this way, then instead of the whole body sliding out, its head would be torn off. To prevent this from happening, the skull contents were removed using some kind of suction device. This collapsed the skull and allowed the fetus to slide out of the womb, pulled gently by the doctor's gloved hands.

I let the pamphlet fall to the floor beside my bed. The TV still muttered in the background. I closed my eyes and considered how it would feel to have my brains sucked out. I went to bed with my clothes on.

Suddenly, it was like a shot went off. My eyes sprang open. I missed him so much that my bones ached. It lasted a few seconds, or was it several minutes? I fell back asleep.

The next day, I had to run to get to work on time. I raced through the doors of Toys-O-Rama, around the small children and piled shopping carts to the back of the store, and then bolted into the break room, where my uniform was in my locker. Because of my jaunt, I was a little sweaty by the time I finally stood in one place long enough to strip out of my winterwear and put on my uniform. My white dress shirt was damp under the armpits and down the centre of my back. I doubted that I smelled very good. I punched in.

A few of my co-workers sat silently in the break room. I didn't say anything to them. Instead I read a scribbled message on a large whiteboard mounted on the wall:

> This break room is DISGUSTING! It is obviously that you live like this at home. (Food on the floor.) Paper airplanes all over the floor. This stops NOW! If not, the break room will be closed to everyone. Same for washrooms.
>
> Management

I headed for the front of the store, where the cashier supervisor told me I was on register five.

My first customer of the day was a woman with blood-red hair, thick eye makeup, and black lipstick. She was buying three miniature sports cars, two WWE action figures, and a

– 28 –

Scrabble game.

"Can I get you a gift receipt for any of these items?" I asked.

"Um, yes," she said.

"Which items?"

"All of them."

"Together on the same receipt? Or separated?"

"I don't know. What's a gift receipt?"

"A gift receipt is a receipt without the price on it, which is good for an exchange or store credit."

"So I can't return it?"

"Not with the gift receipt."

"I thought I had forty-five days after Christmas to make a return."

"With a regular receipt, but not with a gift receipt."

"So why would I want a gift receipt?"

"The gift receipt is only if you won't see the person after you give them the gift and you don't want them to know how much it cost."

"Huh?"

"You can give them the receipt at the same time as the gift, and they can exchange it on their own."

"Oh. No, I don't think I want a gift receipt."

"Okay," I said. I rang in her purchases. She paid and left.

Later, a chunky middle-aged couple wearing matching winter coats came to my till. They were buying a karaoke machine and a toy dog that barked and did back flips. I rang in their purchases and then tried to up-sell them on some batteries.

"I don't know." The man looked to his female companion. "Honey, don't you have batteries at home?"

"Yeah," the woman said. "For my vibrator." The couple threw their heads back in laughter. The man slapped his thick thigh.

I put my head down and tried to fit their extra-large purchases into some extra-large bags behind the teeny-tiny counter.

"What is it, four AAs?" the man asked his companion and laughed harder. "Kathy," the man said, reading my name tag and abbreviating, "do you always blush like that?"

"Yeah, I blush."

"Or are you just upset because yours takes

five AAs?" He laughed again.

I smiled politely.

"Gary," said his lady friend, "leave the poor girl alone."

"Well, at least there's been a little excitement in your day," the man said. I handed him back his credit card, and they left the store.

I decided I was going to take a break. I'd call the cashier supervisor and tell her I had cramps or some other kind of internal bleeding. I picked up the phone at my till, dialled 800, didn't wait for the pause, and ended up making a page that said, "—ive-seven please. Jane, two-five-seven." I then slammed the phone's handset down without hitting the release button, and the phone fell off the wall onto my cash register, causing it to make a long beeping noise.

The slamming noise played throughout the store but was absorbed into the bright plastic toys piled to the ceiling, surrounding me on all sides. Then the Christmas carols came back on. These songs were fed in from some satellite in Denver, where head office decided what to play in all the Toys-O-Ramas everywhere, so that if you ever found yourself in two Toys-O-Ramas at the same time, it wouldn't be the defiance of physics that struck you first, it would be the synchronicity of the tunes. But that would still not make them good tunes.

Team Players

From her workstation at the Tele-Markup telemarketing office, Tanya Burke watched Gemma Blake enter the room. Gemma held her elbows high while her long legs scissored back and forth, stiffly and quickly, so that she looked like she was nearing the finish line in a speed walking competition. She held her head high in the air as her chunky heels plunked heavily against the floor and her long trench coat swished rhythmically against her striding arms. Gemma really *arrived* at work in the morning.

Tanya Burke did not like Gemma Blake and thought that when she entered the Tele-Markup office space, her tall body and dyed-blonde hair, along with her lanky arms and legs, made her look like a female version of the Scarecrow from *The Wizard of Oz*. Gemma spoke in a sharp voice, and Tanya marvelled at how she always had something pressing to talk about, even first thing in the morning.

"Third one today!" Gemma said, entering the office with her travel mug in the air, then taking a massive swig of coffee. She looked at the clock on the wall. "And it's only a quarter to nine." She took another gulp. "It's all I'm running on. Been up since four a.m."

Gertrude Baker, one of the oldest telemarketers at the Tele-Markup call centre, walked towards Gemma and the office's complimentary coffee station. "How are you, Gemma?" she asked.

"Great!" replied Gemma, pulling her coffee mug away from her mouth. "Two big poops this morning."

From halfway down the long narrow room, Tanya swivelled around to face Gemma, her pregnant belly nearly resting on the chair's padding between her legs. She rolled her eyes, by now familiar with this kind of talk. "Jesus fucking Christ," she muttered, making eye contact with Gertrude as they both shook their heads.

"After a two-day dry spell," Gemma continued, nodding her head, standing next to Gertrude at the coffee station while Gertrude poured herself a cup. "Top me up a little there, will you?" Gemma took the lid off her cup and then thrust it at Gertrude. "I'm telling you. Kids! Had me so worried. I was asking myself, 'Do you go to the doctor about something like that?' I mean, where the heck was she putting it all?"

Gertrude walked back to her carrel while Gemma continued to stand and gesticulate with her one empty hand. She turned and kept talking to Tanya. "But nothing left to worry about. Starting at four a.m. this morning, she made two nice, big, wet poops!"

"Wonderful," Tanya said, shaking her head. Their co-worker Cindy entered the office and sat at the workstation beside Tanya's.

"That's my girl!" Gemma said. Then she walked closer to where Tanya and Cindy sat. "So, as a goal for today," she began, "I'd like to see us all try and up those numbers. I was thinking it might help productivity if we tried to talk less while we were at our desks. I mean, I have no problem at all with talking in the break room, the hallway. No, no, no, no, no, no, no, no! That's A-okay with me. But I was thinking that while we're at our desks, we could try and keep our thoughts to ourselves. That way we'd be extra fired up to talk when a call comes in. How about it?" She nodded furiously, and Tanya sensed that she was supposed to feel enthusiastic about these plans.

"Does this come from management?" Tanya asked.

"Nope," Gemma said. Tanya and Cindy glanced at each other, frowning. "Nope. I was just thinking on my way to work, trying to come up with some new strategies. You know, to *crunch* the numbers. To help *sell*." Gemma laughed and punched the air in front of her. "Oh! Maybe we can even make a game out of it. Like whoever talks the least in between phone calls can get an extra ten minutes on their coffee break? Or maybe everyone else in the office can give them a dollar at the end of the week? How's that sound?"

Tanya and Cindy smiled, then turned around without answering and tried to ignore Gemma until she finally walked away. She went into her office at the back of the room and closed the door behind her.

Tanya stroked her belly, then looked at Cindy and said, "That bitch is fucking insane."

"She is out of control!" Cindy said. "Why does she always want to try out these new ideas? It's like she's kissing management's ass all the time, trying to impress them."

"And if I hear one more thing about her kids..." Tanya scoffed. Tanya was seven months pregnant, but if there was one thing she dreaded talking about, it was children. When she found out that she was pregnant and that the father was going to be no help at all, Tanya took a second job at Tele-Markup to supplement her income as a waitress. Her first trimester had been so physically exhausting that she could barely keep up with all the orders at the restaurant, so she soon gave up that job and made Tele-Markup her sole employment. Since Gemma started working there thirteen weeks ago, Tanya had grown to detest her constant anecdotes about her children. She felt that Gemma was secretly entering both of them into a Best Mom competition. Tanya, who was twenty-eight, single, and broke, felt she had no chance of winning that competition and resented being entered into it in the first place.

Tanya and Cindy sat at their neighbouring desks, fiddling with some papers, when their co-worker Ashley entered the office. Her hair was in a messy ponytail, and her eyes were still puffy from sleep.

"My cousin here yet?" Ashley asked as she sat down. Ashley's cousin, who was also named Ashley, also worked as a telemarketer at the call centre.

"Nope," Cindy replied. Then her phone started ringing. "Jesus fuck. It's early, isn't it?"

"I guess it's nine o'clock wherever that call's going to," Tanya said.

Tele-Markup specialized in cold calls. The phone rang at a marketer's desk, and when she picked it up, it was also ringing at some unknown location. It was the marketer's job to sell rolls of credit card receipt paper to whoever answered the phone.

Cindy picked up her phone and, after a short pause, said, "Hello, and how are you today? Fantastic. May I speak to the person in charge of major purchases?"

Tanya had briefly interviewed for the job

twenty-one weeks ago, and Jake, the man who Gemma had replaced, had assured her that they were providing people with something that they *needed*, saving them the time of having to worry about their receipt paper. "This is a job you can be proud of," Jake had assured her. Tanya had tried to keep a straight face. She'd only needed a job that would pay her and preferred one that was physically undemanding. Jake was later fired.

The company's explanation for firing Jake was that they were going in a different direction. They didn't want anyone to feel "nervous" or "alarmed" by the high number of dismissals that had happened recently. Shortly after Jake's dismissal, a memo was sent out:

> *We understand that some of you may be concerned about the recent changes in our management structure. We are here to answer your questions.*
>
> Sincerely,
> Management

"It's so good of them to clear things up, isn't it?" Cindy said to Tanya when they both received the memo. Soon, other memos arrived:

Reading in between phone calls should consist only of picture-heavy magazines. Thick books, such as novels and short story collections, are no longer allowed. Additionally, playing board games at your desk is no longer permitted. This includes tic-tac-toe.

Thank you,
Management

Next, memos were done away with to keep costs down, and instead notes were handwritten on a whiteboard in the middle of the telemarketers' shared office:

Due to threat of injury, knitting and crochet needles are no longer allowed on the premises. Furthermore, drawing at your desks is no longer permitted.

Thank you for your co-operation,
Management

"What the fuck?" Tanya had yelled, reading the board. "How am I going to get junior's wardrobe ready on time if I can't crochet between calls?" She rubbed her belly and then sat back down at her carrel.

The following Monday, the Tele-Markup telemarketing staff walked into their office to find another note written on the whiteboard:

> After some consideration, it has been decided that while drawing in between phone calls is unacceptable, doodling will be permitted.
>
> > Thank you,
> > Management

"So what," Ashley had said, "are they going to hire a fine arts graduate to keep an eye on us?"

Tanya thought about Ashley's remark later, after finding out that the company had in fact hired someone with a fine arts degree to take over Jake's job. It was as though the company had beaten them to the punchline. On

Gemma Blake's first day, management wrote a welcome for her on the whiteboard:

> Please join us in welcoming our new team manager, Gemma Blake. Gemma comes to us with a background in sculpture and painting from York University. Gemma will be the local authority on the difference between doodles and drawings, as some of you were concerned as to how to tell the difference. We look forward to working with you, Gemma!
>
> Management

Tanya had opted not to welcome Gemma because she distrusted managers and was happier ridiculing them from afar than actually speaking to them. But other women at Tele-Markup had asked Gemma about herself, and Tanya heard from them that after she'd finished school, Gemma married a doctor, had two babies, and was very eager to get back to work for the first time since before she had her kids. She'd been bored at home. She described herself as a "doer." That's when it became clear to Tanya that Gemma had this job because she wanted it, not because she needed it.

"I guess spending Dr. Husband's fat cheques got a little boring for her," Tanya had speculated while talking to Ashley's cousin.

Ashley's cousin had laughed and rolled her eyes.

That was thirteen short weeks ago, during which time Tanya repeatedly overheard Gemma saying, "I just *love* my job. I. Just. *Love it!*" Gemma got to work early. She left on time, but only because the kids needed to be picked up from the babysitter's, she said. Otherwise, Gemma Blake said, she would have gladly worked late.

But lately, there was little need to put in extra work. The calls had slowed down at Tele-Markup.

The same day as Gemma's big poop announcement, and shortly after Ashley arrived at work, Ashley's cousin Ashley entered the office almost twenty minutes late. She was wearing a ponytail twice as messy as her cousin's, and she had a couple of deep red blotches on her neck.

"Is it love this time, Ash?" Ashley asked her cousin.

"*Shh!*" Ashley's cousin replied. "I can't believe the marks this guy left."

Tanya and Cindy laughed at the Ashleys, then the four women stared at their phones, hoping they would ring and dreading they would ring. Ashley's cousin's phone rang and she picked it up.

"Hello, may I please speak to the person in charge?" Ashley's cousin talked like a robot on the phone. "When would be a good time to call back? Yes, thank you. Goodbye."

Ashley leaned back two desks over. "Ash, you've got to put your hips in to it," she said.

"What the fuck does that mean?" Ashley's cousin replied.

From her office, Gemma Blake was yelling, "I would *kill* for my kids! *Kill* for them!"

"Is she on her personal phone?" Cindy asked Tanya, then directed her attention to the latest whiteboard note. Tanya hadn't noticed that it had been updated. It read:

Personal video game devices and cellular phones are not to be used in the office between phone calls. Please refrain from bringing them into the work area at all.

Thank you,
Management

"Who's going to tell the warden?" Tanya asked.

Cindy's phone rang. She picked it up and then paused. "Yes, hello? Am I speaking with the person in charge? I just guessed. I mean, you *sounded* like the person in charge." Cindy talked like a phone sex operator. She had the highest number of sales.

"*That's* what I mean," said Ashley to her cousin.

Cindy hung up. She looked over at Tanya and the Ashleys. They all sat looking at their phones.

"How many calls have you been making lately?" Tanya asked.

"Half as many as last week," Cindy replied.

"Layoffs are coming," Ashley's cousin said.

"Shit."

Gemma came over to where they were sitting. "Hey, girls," she said, looking down from where she stood behind them. "You've spent a little time talking." She frowned in concern. "Everything okay?" She spread her fingers apart and then waved her hand around in front of the women. "Anything I need to know about?" She looked back and forth between them. "Anything you want to share?"

Tanya snorted. "We were just wondering how to go about ordering in our lunch now that cell phones have been banned." Cindy and the Ashleys turned to look at Gemma.

Gemma's face dropped. "Pardon me?" she asked.

"Take a look." Tanya directed her gaze to the whiteboard. Gemma read carefully.

"That's fine," she said, straightening her blouse. "I'm sure it's still okay to use cell phones in the break room."

"You're sure?" Cindy said. "We wouldn't want to get in trouble if management caught us."

"I'll double check, but I'm quite sure," Gemma said. Gemma spent most of her day on the phone with her kids, and her voice carried from her office into the workspace. Once ·the loud conversation was done, Gemma would then repeat segments of it to the rest of the office. "Jeffrey wants to know why we can't have a swimming pool in the living room!" Gemma would laugh uproariously. Others in the office who listened would laugh politely, then return to work.

"Might be hard for some of us to get by without cell phones in the office," Tanya said, looking at Gemma. Cindy and the Ashleys turned back to their phones and tried to look busy.

"It's different for mothers," Gemma explained. "It's not like I'm just goofing off on the phone. My kids need to *always* be able to reach me. *Always!*" Gemma looked at Tanya's belly. "When are you due?" she asked.

"June eighth. Seven weeks."

"Seven weeks, Tanya Burke. Then you'll see. Your cell phone will become a little more important to you then." Gemma walked away.

The next day at work, the complimentary coffee station had disappeared. A note on the whiteboard read:

> *Due to cutbacks, staff are encouraged to enjoy a beverage from the snack wagon in the parking lot.*
>
> *Thank you for your co-operation,*
>
> *Management*

Tanya and Cindy stared at the board.

"Are pregnant chicks even supposed to drink coffee?" Cindy asked. Gemma had come in behind her and overheard.

"My doctor says one cup a day—" Tanya began.

"No, sir*ee!* No caffeine for expecting mommies!" Gemma boomed, looking past Cindy and Tanya at the board. "Okay, so it looks like the coffee's gone now too." She looked as sad as she had the day before, when cell phones were banned. She took a deep breath and straightened her shoulders. She walked with her head high as she returned to her office.

"Everyone," Tanya started, looking in the direction of Gemma's office, "is a fucking ex-

pert on what pregnant women should do!"
She walked up to the whiteboard and used
her index finger to erase the *cou* in *encouraged*.
Cindy pointed out that the same thing could
be done by removing the last half of *enjoy* and
the first half of *beverage*, although the large
gap in between made it more difficult to see
the final word. Two other women in the office erased some letters and deformed others,
so that the sign soon read: *Due to cocks, staff
are enraged to enrage from the crack wagon in the
puking lot. Hand job operation, Man.*

"That felt good," Tanya said. She turned
to Cindy, and they smiled at each other before returning to their workstations. Then,
both Ashleys walked through the door together.

"What's a 'hand job operation'?" Ashley's
cousin asked. They were nearly twenty minutes late, but most of the women in the office
were too busy laughing to notice.

That same day, when it was time to go for a
coffee break, Tanya declined. The Ashleys and
Cindy went downstairs to the parking lot, but

Tanya decided to wait at her desk. She had recently been going over some breathing exercises with her mom, and she wanted to practice. With the coffee station gone, the office nearly emptied out at break time.

Tanya closed her eyes and began to quietly practice her controlled inhalations, followed by many short rapid exhalations. She began to feel lightheaded but wanted to practice while she could. She didn't like talking about the birth with anyone, not even her mom, because she was so scared of the pain she would feel. Yesterday, someone had mentioned the need to "tear" herself away from the novel she was reading, and Tanya had winced. Lately, she had been clinging to her breathing exercises, convincing herself that this would cure her of any discomfort during childbirth.

In the middle of one exercise, Tanya began to sense that someone was watching her. Her eyes popped open, and she turned to see Gemma looking at her.

"You're practicing your Lamaze?" Gemma asked.

Tanya nodded, feeling irritated that Gemma watched her doing her breathing exercises. She did not share Gemma's enthusiasm for motherhood and did not want to talk to her about the so-called miracle of childbirth.

But to Tanya's surprise, Gemma didn't try to talk about labour. All she said was, "Every little bit helps." Then she put a cup of steaming tea on Tanya's table. "I really liked this when I was preggers." Gemma smiled. "I've got a kettle in my office. Don't go telling everyone or I'll never get any quiet in there. But this tea is really soothing and totally safe for the baby."

Tanya said, "Thank you," but it sounded like a question.

"No worries," Gemma said. "I'll bet they wouldn't have *that* at the snack wagon." Gemma walked back to her office. Before closing the door behind her, she stuck her head out and said to Tanya, "Lamaze is good, but *take the drugs!*" She smiled, then hopped into her office and closed the door.

Tanya thought about walking to the bathroom and throwing the tea into the toilet. But it smelled delicious, and no one else was around to see her, so she drank it instead.

After the morning coffee break, the work picked up slightly. Ashley's phone rang. "Hello, may I please speak to the person in charge of major purchases?"

Tanya leaned back and looked at Ashley's cousin, who still had traces of red hickies on one side of her neck. "Don't get into the same position I'm in, Ash," she said, pointing at her stomach.

"I'm careful," said Ashley's cousin.

"Hello, sir. How are you doing today?" Ashley said.

"Be carefuller," said Tanya. "Because it happens—" She raised her hand above her head and snapped her fingers. "—like that!"

"I am calling to enquire about the status of your credit card receipt paper."

"I haven't had sex in thirteen months," said Cindy.

Tanya and Ashley's cousin looked at her. Ashley looked over at her also, with her phone held to her ear.

"We are the leading suppliers of credit card receipt rolls in the United States and Mexico," Ashley said, still staring at Cindy.

"I'm going to be thirty next month,"

explained Cindy. "It gets harder as you get older. To meet people." She looked at the Ashleys. "You'll see."

Then the phones starting ringing, and the women were busy at work.

At lunchtime that day, Tanya snuck to the break room with her brown bag in hand. She was trying to save money by packing a lunch, and also trying to increase her culinary skills, but she didn't want the other women in the office to notice that she wasn't part of any of the small groups heading out for lunch. She'd been ridiculed recently by Cindy and the Ashleys for bringing an egg salad sandwich to work. Tanya had been so happy with herself for making a simple packed lunch that she showed the halved sandwich to Cindy and both Ashleys.

"Not exactly a moon landing, is it?" Cindy had said to Ashley's cousin, presumably thinking that Tanya could not hear. Tanya walked away slightly hurt but knew that she would have said the same thing if Cindy had come in bragging about her own lunch. The sarcasm in the office was relentless.

Today, Tanya brought her smoked turkey wrap, Fig Newtons, and apples into the break room to eat them for lunch. She'd spent a lot of time thinking about and preparing this meal, but she knew by looking at it that she'd be hungry again in less than an hour and running out to one of the snack wagons in the parking lot at her next coffee break.

The break room was laid out like a galley kitchen, with a toaster oven, a bar fridge, a small sink, and a drying rack organized along one wall, and a small couch and two folding chairs backed against the other. Whenever she sat on the couch, Tanya felt like she was either on a car ride or sitting in a tiny movie theatre, watching a tableau of kitchen appliances.

But their office building was located in a small enclave of office buildings, and there was little else in the neighbourhood. There was an Irish-style pub across the street, but it didn't open until four p.m. A few snack wagons and cafeteria-style establishments were set up in the parking lots and ground floors of some of the neighbouring office buildings, but very few of them provided anywhere to sit.

Many of Tanya's co-workers sat at their desks and ate their lunch, but Tanya thought that was depressing, and it made the small break from work feel like no break at all. The break room was far from perfect but still the best of the limited options available.

When Tanya turned to enter the break room, she saw Gemma Blake sitting on the small couch with her arm extended over the back of the seat next to her. Her tall body seemed to fill the entire space. Tanya winced in Gemma's direction and then unpacked her lunch at the counter. She sat on one of the folding chairs and began to eat her turkey wrap.

"Not much of a lunch," Gemma said, pointing with her chin at the three apples and half dozen cookies sitting on the counter.

"I'm not much of a cook," Tanya said.

"I wasn't either until I had kids," Gemma said.

"Hmm." Tanya didn't know how much she cared to have a conversation with Gemma.

"I used to love Kraft Dinner and hot dogs." Gemma chuckled and shook her head slowly from side to side. "I mean, *come on!* Kraft Dinner, sheesh." Tanya and Gemma both stared forward at the narrow kitchenette. Tanya wondered why Gemma wasn't eating in her office today, then assumed it was probably the same reason why she wasn't eating at her own desk.

Gemma crossed her legs, extending her top leg in front of her, and began to examine her shoe. Then she looked over at Tanya, who was almost done her turkey wrap and not even close to full.

"I should have made ten of these," Tanya said. Gemma laughed.

"Here." She pulled half a corned beef sandwich out of her purse. Tanya saw that there was almost two inches of meat on the sandwich and that a thick daub of mustard spilled over the sliced edge and was smeared against the plastic wrap. Her mouth watered. But she wondered why Gemma was offering her this.

"I'm okay," Tanya said. "Once I eat the apples." She looked over at the counter. "I was only kidding."

Gemma looked at her and then started

talking in a soft voice, one Tanya had never heard before. "I'm only giving this to you because I can't finish it and it won't be any good by tomorrow. Someone should eat it." She placed it on the counter beside the rest of Tanya's lunch. "My mother-in-law made the corned beef. I never cooked until I had kids, but I never said I got good at it."

Tanya smiled. Gemma had just told her a joke, or something like a joke. For one moment, Gemma had become warm.

Tanya saw that Gemma had her cell phone in her right hand, held against her lap. Gemma must have seen her looking at it.

"We're not supposed to have these in the workspace, so I decided to come in here for lunch, just in case my kids' school or my husband has to get a hold of me," Gemma explained. "It's my job to make sure no one else uses them at work, so I can't be caught with one, or who'd take me seriously?" The sharp tone that Tanya associated with Gemma was returning as she talked about her authoritative role at the office. "It's a tough rule, though, when you're worried about your kids all day. Makes me *sick* with worry not to have this thing in my hand."

"There should be different rules for parents," Tanya offered, and she realized that she didn't know if she was being sarcastic or not.

Gemma huffed. "That'll be the day." Once again, the sarcasm was unclear. Gemma's face went slack as she stared at the toaster oven and kicked her foot nervously in front of her. Tanya could tell that she was thinking about something outside of Tele-Markup. Her kids, most likely, but maybe something else instead. Tanya reached out and grabbed the corned beef sandwich on the counter. Perhaps it had been given to her in charity, but until she learned how to pack a proper lunch, it was charity she needed. Her stomach dictated so much of her life these days.

"Thanks for the sandwich," Tanya said, looking at Gemma.

"Believe it or not," Gemma said, standing and straightening her skirt, "women like us are on the same team." She turned and left the break room.

Tanya unwrapped the sandwich and took a large bite. The mustard was tangy, and the corned beef was soft and salty. The back of her mouth watered even as she chewed. She wished for a mother-in-law, or a husband who might call her on her cell phone. She tried not to think about it as she finished her half of the sandwich.

"Fucking hormones," she muttered to herself as she wiped her eyes and stared at the toaster oven across from her.

"I think we need a drink, ladies," Tanya said to Cindy and the Ashleys after work that day. They all looked at her. "I'm having soda water, don't worry."

They went to the Irish pub. They sat down and got their drinks.

Cindy looked at Tanya. "Why'd you keep it?" Tanya glared at Cindy, unsmiling. "Look, we've all been wondering. And since who knows how much longer we'll all be working together, why not just say?"

Tanya took a sip of her soda, then shrugged her shoulders and leaned back in her chair. "I kept it because I didn't know what to do. I had no one to talk to. I couldn't figure it out. And it took me so long to decide, that it was too late and there was no decision left to make."

"But you're happy now?"

"Happy in a terrified-out-of-my-mind kind of way. But when he kicks, it's cool. I like to think he's feisty."

The women drank silently for a few minutes.

"I don't care if they lay me off," Ashley's cousin said while looking around the pub. "I bet I could get a waitressing job or something. Probably pays way more."

Tanya nodded.

"God, did you see Gemma's face when she saw that the coffee station was gone?" Ashley's cousin asked. "I thought she was going to cry."

"She's such a bitch," Ashley said.

Tanya placed her glass on the table. "She's just pissed off like the rest of us. What do you think management's going to write on that board tomorrow? 'From now on, please bring your own toilet paper.' Or maybe we'll be sitting on each other's laps to conserve chairs." Tanya took a sip of her soda water.

The women were silent.

"Gemma's more like us than she is like the management," Tanya continued. "It's more like we're all on the same team." Gemma's words felt strange in Tanya's mouth, but she'd wanted to use them.

"Fuck that," said Ashley's cousin, slamming down her empty pint glass and flagging the waiter. "Gemma's not like us."

"Exactly," said Ashley, after finishing her drink as well. "When we all get canned, guess who'll just go back to being a doctor's wife? Won't be us, will it?"

Tanya looked away, sensing that the Ashleys were right, but still she felt a pang of sympathy for Gemma. She was beginning to sense the hardship behind Gemma's ability to smooth her appearance even when something bothered her. Where had she learned that? And she imagined Gemma's mother-in-law, preparing beautiful corned beef dinners, while Gemma stood ineptly to the side, never having learned how to cook. Cindy and the Ashleys couldn't explain Lamaze techniques to Tanya. In fact, they would have surely made fun of Tanya if they ever caught her practicing. Words such as *tearing* and *breathing exercises* were as abstract to them as *hand job operations*. Tanya had to admit that her future could end up resembling Gemma Blake's—and that maybe it would be alright if it did.

Ashley's cousin was snapping her fingers in front of Tanya's face. "Yo, T, where'd you go?"

Tanya shook her head. "I was just thinking about how much I want a scotch."

"I'll have one for you," Ashley said, rubbing Tanya's arm. She raised her hand in the air and called out, mockingly, "*Garçon!*"

The next day, the layoffs started, just as the four women had suspected. But there was still a surprise in store. A messenger from head office was inside Gemma Blake's office.

"Me? What?" Gemma yelled from inside her office. "I don't understand."

The layoffs came from upstairs. If she had questions, she could speak to them. The messenger left the Tele-Markup office, and then Gemma staggered into the middle of the room.

"I love my job." She looked down at a

small pink paper in her hands. Her eyes filled with tears, and she ran out of the room, her chunky heels clicking noisily as she left.

"Not as satisfying as I'd thought it'd be," said Cindy. Tanya felt like she was on the verge of tears. "T, you okay?" Cindy asked.

Tanya sniffled as tears pooled in her eyes. "Fucking hormones." She got up and followed Gemma out of the office.

Gemma was sitting on the front steps of the office building that housed Tele-Markup. Tanya still wasn't sure why she'd followed Gemma out of the office, but she felt compelled to sit beside her. For a moment, she thought about touching Gemma's arm, but she didn't.

"It doesn't make any sense, Gemma," she said. "It's just because they're a fucked-up company."

Gemma sniffled and looked at Tanya. "Are you going to keep up the language once you have that baby?"

Tanya pulled away. "Seriously?"

Gemma started crying again. "I know! I'm sorry! Kids are my life, though. I can't help it."

The two of them sat on the steps, watching the traffic out on the street.

"It's not like I ever thought I would be a famous artist," Gemma sobbed, "but maybe an art history teacher, or a gallery owner. I used to look down on women like me, who stayed at home, looking after a husband and kids."

"There's no reason to be unhappy with what you've got," Tanya said, remembering all the times she'd fought off feelings of fear and loneliness when she thought about single parenthood. "You did it the way you're supposed to. Marriage *then* babies. And you don't even need this job. I heard your husband is a doctor."

"I *felt* like I needed this job. Carl's a doctor, yeah, but—" She looked out into the street. "He gets to leave the house every day and go to the hospital and be his own person." She wrung her hands. "And I'm with those kids..." she trailed off. "I love my kids."

"No one's doubting that," said Tanya, rolling her eyes and rubbing Gemma's shoulder.

"But *I* want to be my own person for a change."

"Well, Jesus," Tanya said. "There've got to be better places to do that than Tele-Markup."

Gemma snorted. "Not when you haven't worked in five years. Well—" She made air quotes with her fingers. "*Worked.*"

Even though part of her felt like she needed to protect her personal information by keeping it secret, Tanya decided to talk to Gemma in the hopes that it might comfort her. "This was the only job I could get. I applied for so many. I act like I don't need it, but I do. I really, really do. I couldn't keep the job I had when I got pregnant, and no one wants to hire you once you're showing. They know you'll be gone soon, I guess, or they don't want to get saddled with your maternity pay and shit." Tanya smiled at Gemma. "I mean, your maternity pay and *stuff.*"

"You need to marry a doctor," Gemma said, laughing.

"Hilarious," Tanya said.

They both stared at the traffic again.

"I'll help you pack up your stuff," Tanya offered, "but I'm not supposed to lift anything."

"This is a blessing in disguise, I guess,"

Gemma said, standing and straightening her blazer. "Something better is going to come along, I'll bet."

Gemma and Tanya pulled open the office building's heavy doors and headed back inside.

The Falls Side

It wasn't exactly my dream in life to be a house-keeper, or chambermaid, or whatever, but I was pretty messed up over my recent breakup with Charlie, the saddest I'd ever been actually. I was also broke and also living with my mom again, so Shannon got me a job at her work when I moved back to Niagara Falls, Ontario, our hometown. It was just like old times. Shannon and I started seeing each other every day, and I knew there were things about this job that I'd miss after I'd moved on. Since Shannon was going through a divorce while I was dealing with a breakup of my own, we had lots to talk about, which is always a plus when you've got a crappy job to do.

"You're the fastest, you two; that's why I

asked you," our manager, Donatella, had told us, but in fact, that was not true. She'd asked us of all people because she was a fifty-five-year-old lesbian who was hot for Shannon and was trying to kiss up a little. Shannon was not interested but played her cards so that her tardiness, extra smoke breaks, and the odd stolen housecoat went unnoticed by Donatella. This meant, however, that Donatella saw me as the "other woman," which was fine because her dislike of me did not outweigh her attraction to Shannon, and so Shannon got enough perks to go around. I figured one day Shannon might score me a housecoat too.

"Je-ee-ee-sus," Donatella said after letting us into room 916. "Some people, hey girls? Some people." She thumbed the collar of a men's wool jacket that was hung over the back of a chair. "Like money's disposable to them." She took a long look at the mess the room was in. "Put it all in bags, girls, all of it—even the expensive stuff." She looked back at me. "I'll ask security where to put it."

It had happened before where I'd found a drawer full of socks or a bag of makeup in the bathroom, something that got overlooked and left behind. But these people left everything. All their clothes, their bathroom supplies, their shoes and luggage. Piles of magazines and books completely covered the desk. The closet was full of dresses and men's jackets. There was a nightgown on the back of the bathroom door and empty food containers sitting on the piles of junk. The people had lived in this hotel room for just over a week, but it looked like they'd lived there for a month.

I grabbed a bunch of spare garbage bags from my cart and walked to the far end of the room, near the desk, beside the window. The Falls Side Hotel guaranteed everyone who stayed in it a view of the Canadian and American waterfalls, both of them natural wonders of the world. It meant that the hotel was long and thin, with rooms on only one side of the hallway. Every room had virtually the same view of the semi-circular falls and stone walkways and kiosks selling hotdogs and lots of tiny people posing in groups for cameras. After only two months, I rarely did more than glance out the window, quickly, while I was cleaning the far end of the room, and if the curtains were closed, sometimes I just left them closed. The falls had always been there, and I figured they always would be.

"The counter is covered in pill bottles," Shannon yelled from the bathroom.

"Anything good?" I yelled back as I began to fill a garbage bag.

"It's all herbal shit," she said. "No fun."

"Sometimes herbal shit can be fun," I offered.

"Naw," said Shannon. "I'm a mom now anyway. Gotta make good decisions."

The longer I worked with Shannon, the more it seemed to me that she missed the good old days of sitting on her mom's couch, getting high, and planning for a future that wasn't here yet. The first day I slept over at Shannon's, we smoked some hash oil that Shannon's mom's boyfriend had given us and that he'd described as "pretty mediocre." We sat baked on her couch laughing at a porno called *Forrest Hump* that Shannon had found in her mom's closet.

When Shannon and I were baked, we often started talking about the falls, wondering what it would be like to see them as a bird, imagining the feeling of going over in a barrel, figuring that maybe they were the secret centre of the universe. Shannon once said, "Like, okay, so let's say that the waterfall is actually just a microcosm, or a macrocosm, like the way people are always thinking about jumping over it to see what's on the bottom. Well, suppose that our waterfall is just the bottom of another waterfall, and some people jump over it into our world, thinking it will be better than the one they're from, and you could go back up out of it if you just worked it out right in your head." We both used to try to imagine coming from way up above and then crashing down into Niagara Falls, Ontario, the strip with all the wax museums and the three-storey motels and the big hotels that bought up all the land closest to the falls and somehow promised everyone the same view so that no one gets jealous or whatever.

I looked around room 916. "All this is going to go in the garbage?" I moved to the desk and started tossing the magazines and cardboard food containers into a garbage bag. The magazines on the desk were women's fashion magazines, but there were also some copies of *Us* and *People*, the same magazines that Charlie used to read. Beside the desk was a suitcase, completely closed and standing upright. I undid the zippers and peeked inside. It was half full of dirty socks, and there was a cellophane wrapper from a pack of cigarettes. I zipped it back up and leaned the suitcase up against the wall. In the space between the bed and the window, there were three piles of clothes that had been sorted into whites, colours, and darks.

"I guess they were going to wash these before they abandoned them."

"Huh?" Shannon was still throwing out the pill bottles in the bathroom, apparently one at a time, just in case there was anything better than multivitamins or weight-loss supplements.

"Their clothes, they sorted them into piles." There were a couple of sweaters in the colours pile that looked like they would fit me. I picked up a navy blue one, thin with a V-neck. I held it up to my chest and saw that it would sit perfectly on my hips and that the arms would pass my wrists and cuff around my hands, which some people might consider too big, but for me it was ideal. The V-neck in the front made it look fashionable. I so badly wanted to wear something stylish. I felt like all my clothes were too practical; all my clothes were becoming work clothes. "Who do you think they were?" I asked Shannon, throwing the sweater back on top of the pile.

"Who knows?"

"They left *all* their clothes?"

"I don't know. Maybe they have more tucked away in a castle somewhere."

I dropped the garbage bag I was holding and headed into the bathroom. "How many toothbrushes are there?"

"Two. And one tube of Crest whitening toothpaste and a bottle of Chanel face wash."

I picked up the face wash. "This looks expensive."

"Put it in the bag, Denise. It's not worth losing your job over."

"No, I know. I just think—it's so small, they could have easily taken it with them."

"Well, clearly they were in a huge fucking rush." Shannon dragged the garbage bag into the foyer just outside the bathroom door.

I pulled back the curtain on the bathtub and found two damp bathing suits hanging from the showerhead, as well as three opened bars of hotel soap and one bottle of store-bought shampoo. "They also forgot their 'hair growth stimulating shampoo for men.' I'll bet someone's missing that."

Shannon moved back into the bathroom next to me. "Is it weird that there are empty pudding cups *and* five empty bottles of Laker Light?"

"I don't know, is it?"

Shannon looked at me with her eyebrows raised. "Denise, like, he was totally way older than her." She shook her head. "A little *Lolita* action, maybe?"

I made a barfing noise. "Unless the pudding cups were his," I said, putting the swim-suits, shampoo, and little bars of soap into a garbage bag.

"What kind of adult eats pudding cups?"

"The kind who lives in a hotel room for a month."

"Like the *Lolita* guy. Who played him in that movie?"

"Jeremy Irons."

"My mom thinks he's hot."

"Mine too."

"Even though he's a pedophile?"

"Only in the movie."

"This could be the root cause of our problems with men, Denise."

"That our moms like Jeremy Irons?"

"Settle down. You want to clean the bathtub, or should I?"

"You can. I'll do the beds."

"Maybe there wasn't a big age difference," I said as I walked back into the bedroom area. "Or, you know, if there was, she could have still been an adult." I wanted to imagine the couple as happy and loving, the way Charlie and I had once been. Him running her a bath after she'd worked all day, or ordering takeout in advance of her getting home so it would be waiting for her when she got there.

"No, you're right," said Shannon. "No sense getting worked up over nothing."

Then I found a hairbrush on the floor between the two beds, and I gagged a little. "I hate other people's hair." Shannon came into the bedroom, and we both huddled together, looking at the strands inside of the brush's bristles.

"Dyed," said Shannon.

"She was probably in her twenties, at least."

"How old were you when you first dyed your hair?"

"Eighteen. Still, an adult."

"I was twelve."

"What?"

"To piss off my parents. I dyed it mahogany with a box of henna that Jenna Woodhouse's mom picked up in Buffalo."

"Did it wash out?"

"Sort of. But I didn't start *dye-dying* my hair until I was twenty-two. I was waitressing at Wimpy's, and they said the girls on staff had to look nice."

"You didn't get the same memo about this place?" I asked as I scratched my head and stuck out my tongue. The uniforms were powder-blue pants and matching golf-style shirts with white collars and white trim around the breast pocket. But the best part was the blackened knee pads that fit poorly and were too thin to be useful. We looked like a couple of washed-up roller derby queens.

Shannon laughed a little.

"Do you ever talk to Jenna anymore?" I

asked. "Didn't she move out of town?"

"She did, but she's back now," Shannon said. "I saw her at Grumpy's just last Wednesday, and she said she saw Bill Gitlin on the States side two weeks ago. He married an American girl and, *co-in-ci-dent-ally*, he is totally bald."

"And he's young, right?"

"He's older than you'd think."

"So if she's about twenty-two, and he's balding, then that could be totally fine, although it still doesn't explain why they left." I thought about when I had packed a bag and left mine and Charlie's old apartment, how I'd snuck out late one night before he got home from the bar. I pulled hard on the corners of the fitted sheet to get them out from under the mattress. "Maybe she left him and he followed. Or maybe he cheated on her and she found out."

"Maybe he checked his other girlfriend into a room downstairs and thought he could just divide his time here between the two of them."

"No one would really do that."

"Sure they would. Guys are dogs."

"But that?"

"Did you look all the way under the bed? If they left all this out in the open.... It's going to be fucked up under the bed."

We squatted down beside each other and looked under the bed. There were three more magazines, a wool scarf, six or seven empty water bottles, a few dirty spoons, and more clothes. But nothing horrifying.

Shannon pointed at one of the magazines. "Porno?"

"Not sure." I reached my hand under the bed and picked up a magazine. "Yep."

"Sleazeball." Shannon stood up and went back to the bathroom.

"Like you don't read porno."

"Sure, but I already pegged this guy for a perv, and it's different when pervs read porn."

I could see the sharp heels of a pair of black stilettos peeking out from underneath the clothes. I bent down and picked them up. They were three inches high and patent leather. I was good at walking in tall heels. Charlie used to say that the sound of heels clicking against the floor was the sound of attractive women. I thought that maybe if

I had a pair of shoes like these, I might then end up with a reason to wear them. But Niagara Falls was a boring place. I tossed them in the garbage bag.

When I stood up again, my left knee pad fell down to my ankle.

"These knee pads are driving me crazy!" I hollered to Shannon, who was still in the bathroom.

"Yeah, try not wearing knee pads and see how crazy that drives you." Shannon walked out of the bathroom and stood in the middle of the bedroom, next to the television.

"Did you notice my limp?" she asked.

"What limp?"

"So, you didn't notice." Shannon took off both of her rubber gloves and pointed at her right knee.

"Listen to this." She bent her knee several times. "You hear it?"

"No," I said.

"Like Rice Krispies. Did I tell you when I was on my 'separation vacation' last month I decided to go on one of those boat rides under the falls? Something about the mist and the humidity down there or something.

My knee *locks*, freezes right up. I thought it might never go back to normal, like for the rest of my life I wouldn't be able to bend my knee. Did I tell you? And everyone else there is Japanese, so I don't know how I'm supposed to tell them that I'm basically paralyzed. But then it eased up. From this job, Denise. That's what does it."

"But you don't even look like you're limping," I said.

"I totally fucking am. I'll probably need surgery eventually."

"Well, you'll always know when it's about to rain."

"What?"

"Never mind. At least you got a vacation."

"Yeah, but it would have been better if I'd gone away. I feel sorry for tourists who come here. There isn't anything to do, and you just get ripped off all the time." Shannon put her gloves back on. I thought of how I'd always wanted to take Charlie on a boat ride under the falls, but he'd insisted that they were uncomfortable and overpriced. Maybe he'd been right.

"Did I tell you about the guy I met from Mexico at Wimpy's?" Shannon continued.

"He was visiting Niagara Falls with his girl-friend, although I never met the girlfriend. I was talking to him for, like, ten seconds before he told me he had ecstasy in his backpack if I wanted some. Did I tell you? I said, 'No way, Jose!' before I even realized that his name might actually be Jose, but I guess it wasn't. *Then* he tells me he has coke if I'm more into that. I thought about it for a second, since I was on vacation, but no, no, I thought, I'm a mom now, I need to make better decisions, even when I'm on vacation."

"Good for you," I said.

"*Then* he tells me he also has pot, hash, Percocets, and mescaline. In his backpack!"

"And you didn't do any of it?"

"Some pot, just some pot—and only because I was on vacation. It was shit anyway."

"Have you talked to Jeff since you got back from vaca— What the hell?" I had pulled open the drawer of the nightstand between the two beds. There were about fifteen AA batteries in it. "I just don't get it." I turned to Shannon. "Need some batteries?"

"Careful, there are probably about eight different sex toys around here somewhere that go with those batteries. Put your gloves on, Denise."

Shannon limped back to the bathroom, and I moved to the other bed and began to strip off the sheets.

"But I was saying, have you talked to Jeff?"

"I have. We might try couples therapy. I'm still going to stay with my mom for a while though."

"I hope you two can work it out."

"Should I ask you about Charlie?" Shannon said. "Don't tell me if you don't want."

"Charlie and I aren't talking. My lawyer said not to be in contact with him."

"Lawyers. Shit. When did things get so fucking complicated?"

"Seriously." I sprayed the nightstand with cleaner and wiped it down. I tried not to think about Charlie. "Maybe these two were just a couple of daredevils. Maybe they are cramming themselves into a barrel as we speak."

"They were running from the law, I bet."

"Maybe for robbing a casino, or a bank, so they won't need this stuff because they can afford to get all new everything." I turned the lamp on and off to make sure the bulb didn't need replacing. "Maybe they're starting over. Maybe they just had enough of who they were and left it all behind."

"People don't really do that."

"I don't know. They don't do it often, but they might still do it once in a while."

"Well, then they're the suckers."

"They're not suckers, they're—"

"They're suckers because they'll still be their same shitty selves, even without all their stuff. But now they don't even have anything to wear." Shannon came out of the bathroom and threw a half-full garbage bag against the floor. "Denise, I have other rooms to clean later. I don't want to work until midnight."

"Me neither."

"Well, my kid doesn't want me to work until midnight either, so that makes three of us. Neither does my mom, who'll have to babysit her until midnight if that's when I work until, so that makes four."

I looked at the floor and felt my face get hot. "I get it, Shannon," I said without looking up. "Neither of us wants to work until midnight."

Shannon looked at me and then turned away and dumped the waste bin out into a garbage bag. "We still gotta vacuum and do the mirrors."

"We've still got a lot to do before then."

"I know. I was just saying." She moved back into the bathroom, and I heard the faucets turn on. I hated the way that Shannon always brought up her kid, as if being a mother made her time more precious than mine. Charlie didn't want kids, so I said I didn't either and never really thought about it after that, but I used to look at pictures of his niece sometimes because I figured that was sort of what our daughter would look like if we ever had one. So it wasn't like I couldn't even imagine what it was like to have a kid.

I moved over to the entertainment unit and began opening drawers. The first drawer was full, almost to the brim, with men's shirts. Some were dress shirts and others were plain T-shirts, but they were all neatly folded. At the bottom of the drawer, buried under the clothes, was a Lonely Planet guide to New York City. The cover was worn and soft but still held some gloss in its finish. Were they headed there, or had they just been? I'd lived a drive away from New York City my whole life, but I'd never visited once. Charlie had said that we would go, but we never made it. I made sure Shannon was still inside the bathroom, then I stuck the slim guidebook down the back of my pants. My baggy shirt covered the bulge it created.

I opened the next drawer, and it was as tidy as the first. It was full of men's jeans, about five or six pairs. These people were clean when they wanted to be, or maybe they had split personalities, or maybe she was messy and he was neat. Maybe they fought about it and that's why they broke up and left. The basement room where I was staying in my mom's house was so cold and lonely. I used to hate all of the stuff that Charlie left around the apartment, but I hated the thought of it all being gone now.

"Bathroom's done," Shannon said, walking into the bedroom. "Whoa, you alright?"

I sat back on my heels. "I'm fine. I'm just...I'm tired."

She took off her gloves and squatted

beside me.

"I know," she said, and she helped me up.

We emptied out the second drawer together. Then we both moved all of the garbage bags into the hallway and put all of the dirty linen into the hampers. I took two sets of sheets off my cart and walked back into the room. I stood at the foot of the bed and snapped the folded sheet out in front of me. We both watched it float onto the mattress, and then I crouched down beside the bed to tuck the first corner under.

"Careful," Shannon said. "There may be a dead hooker buried in the box spring."

"What?"

"Guilty. These people seem guilty."

"That wouldn't make sense," I said. "Look at all the evidence they'd have left behind." I stuck my hands under the mattress. There was nothing there.

Shannon and I finished making the beds together. I dusted the rest of the furniture while she vacuumed the carpet.

"How long did that take us?" I asked.

Shannon looked at her watch. "Thirty-five minutes. Some of these girls take longer than that just to do the bathroom." Shannon held her right palm up in the air, and we high-fived each other. I grabbed my rags and all-purpose cleaner, and we headed out the door. Before I turned off the light, I gave the room one more glance. We'd made it so that it looked like every other room in the hotel. The beds were perfectly made and totally identical to each other, the carpet was clean, and the furniture was shiny. It was as if those strange customers had never been there. Out the window, I looked at Niagara Falls crashing down outside the hotel. Seeing it from inside room 916, I felt farther away from it than I ever had before. My eyes traced the perimeter of the horseshoe shape, moving away from and then coming back to the walkway in front of the hotel. Next, I looked out past the falls to the border that separated Ontario from New York State. I could feel the travel guide against my skin. I followed Shannon out of the room, turning out the light and closing the door behind us.

Hidden in Plain Sight

You imagine how good it would feel to tell your secret, but something always stops you. You want to get outside yourself and have someone else tell it for you.

Your secret regards Mr. Langford. Mr. Langford is a creep. At the time of his death, your mom tells your dad that Mr. Langford always "rubbed her the wrong way." She hates to say it, but it's true. You feel the same way about him, although your twelve-year-old brain can't articulate your true feelings.

You are eleven. Mr. Langford has a new video camera and decides to test it out by taping things around his yard. He dollies towards the bird bath. He pans across his shrubs. He hoists the camera over the fence and tapes you. You're in your parents' backyard, doing handstands. At dinner that night, you tell your dad.

"Today Mr. Langford videotaped me doing handstands." Your dad drops his fork and looks at you.

"You should tell me, Jessica, when that happens."

You are confused. You *did* tell him, just now. You frown.

After dinner, your dad goes out and knocks on Mr. Langford's door. Your mom tells you to go into the family room and watch television. You are still confused, but you decide it's easier not to ask questions. You watch television, and then you go to bed.

Now it is the following summer, and you are twelve. You have breasts and hips. You are sore with growth, and it seems that everything in your life has changed and gone wrong. You are desperately uncomfortable with your developing body, your height, and your pimples. You do not like any of the looks you receive. You get your period.

"This is going to happen every month," your mother says. She unwraps a maxi pad and shows you how they attach to underwear, how they are disposed of, where she keeps them in the house.

"When will I stop getting it? When will it be over?" You know the answer; you aren't stupid. But you want to hear her say it. You still hope to be wrong.

"Not until you're much older," she says. Your face crumples, and you throw your head into her chest. Change is exhausting.

You are tall. Half a foot taller than the next tallest girl in your homeroom class. The boys look like toddlers compared to you. People can see you no matter where you stand. You despise attention, especially from boys. You attempt invisibility by wearing baggy sweatshirts and Doc Martens. Your look is boyish, though you are not a tomboy, just desperate not to be a girl, not now. You keep your hair long and let it hang in front of your face, which sprouts new pimples daily, glowing like a beacon atop the lighthouse that is your body.

Your parents' house is the only place you can hide. You live on the outskirts of town, near the place where a new airport is being built. The cornfield that used to be in the front of your house is almost gone now. You love the backyard, which is closed in by a high fence. You love to play there by yourself.

It is just after noon, and the sun is high, but there is a cool breeze. The sky is ice blue. The knotted fence posts surround you like armour. You kick your soccer ball against the fence. Your shorts are tight against your body. You're about to outgrow them, but you haven't yet. On the other side of the fence, Mr. Langford stands on a ladder. He is installing lattice along the top of his fence.

You kick the ball into the air, trying to see how high it will go. Your dad can throw the ball into the air and then bounce it off his head. You give it a try. The ball hits you hard and hurts your head. Your eyes fill with tears. You sniffle, holding them back, and then look around for the ball.

"It's over here," Mr. Langford says from the top of his ladder. "You'll have to get it yourself. I'm not going up and down this ladder a hundred times because you can't be bothered to be more careful."

Now, you move towards the gate, where you can get into his yard and retrieve your soccer ball.

You're on his property. You still can't see where the ball has gone. His yard is bigger than your parents', and his is sprinkled with shrubs and trees, potted plants, and gnomes. There is a bird bath and feeder next to the large porch that he built last summer. You see the soccer ball peeking out from beside the porch.

Run over and grab it. You have it between your hands, the thing you came for.

The gate swings shut behind you, and Mr. Langford is standing beside his ladder. Why did he come down? Hadn't he made you retrieve your own ball just so he wouldn't have to do that? He steps towards you, and you get nervous, so you move towards the gate.

"Wait just a minute," he says. Pause. "Turn around and look at me." Do as you are told, holding the ball with both hands in front of you. Look down at his lawn. It is even and flat. It is green like the garter snakes that get into your parents' garage. Move your eyes up to meet his. He checks you out, looks you up and down, and you think that he is also licking his lips. Think about the time with the video camera. Mr. Langford registers differently now. See him the way your father does. You are a tall girl with hips and breasts, with bra straps and maxi pads. And you hate that. You want to be alone and invisible, and no one will let you. You are angry.

Mr. Langford climbs halfway up the ladder and begins poking the lattice. Throw the soccer ball at Mr. Langford. He turns quickly and catches the ball, then wobbles on the ladder. He is about to fall, but he hangs on. He lets go of the ball and it rolls back to you, near the gate. He looks down at you from the ladder.

"That's all, Jessica. You can go," he says. Bend down and pick up the ball, feel your tight shorts stretch across your bottom. Look up, through your legs, to Mr. Langford, upside down. He is upside down and staring at your bum. Stand up. Look Mr. Langford in the eye. Cock your head to one side and drop your hip; take on a coquettish posture that you've seen before, somewhere else.

He looks surprised for a moment. He is about to say something. He turns to face you. His foot slips from the rung, and he spins to try and catch himself. This time, he more than wobbles. Watch him fall. It takes only a few seconds.

Walk over to where he is. Look down at him while he bleeds against the concrete path that rims the perimeter of his yard.

After a long moment, you run inside and tell your dad that Mr. Langford fell off his ladder. You explain that you saw the entire thing from where you kicked your ball in your parents' yard. Soon, the entire neighbourhood is consoling you for having had to witness such a thing.

Everyone thinks that Mr. Langford died an accidental death. Your parents never discover the truth. No one knows about the neighbourhood's little murderer. You are hidden, invisible, even while you stand in plain sight.

The Baby Section

As I walked through the parking lot towards my work, the red, blue, and yellow façade of Toys-O-Rama grew until it loomed over my head. I looked up and saw the grey sky, the tiny speeding snowflakes, and the massive plastic panelling with a smiling zebra smiling out. The sliding doors were held open by my presence as I stood in front of them, staring up at the sky.

"In or out!" Inside the doors, Carly was lining shopping carts up against a wall. "In or out, Kath. I'm fucking freezing," she said, slamming one cart into the back end of the row.

"How's it going, Carly?" She looked at me and then shaped her hand into a gun and motioned like she was shooting herself in the temple. I put my head down and pulled the waist of my too-small winter coat down, sensing that my belly was protruding. My mom had told me that morning that I looked like I'd put on weight since I'd moved back home. She said she'd told me just in case I wanted to do something about it, not to make me feel bad.

I turned towards Pam, who was talking on the phone behind the customer service desk. When she saw me, she hung up the receiver and held her hand out towards me, palm up, and gestured with her fingers for me to approach her. Throughout the large box-shaped store, Christmas carols played and fluorescent lights glowed.

"Laura," Pam said, looking at me.

I looked to my left and to my right.

"Laura," Pam said again.

"Me?" I pointed at myself.

"Uh-huh."

"My name's Kathleen."

"Huh?" Pam scrunched up her face.

"I'm Kathleen," I repeated.

She shook her head. "Sorry, hon. Look, I

just got off the phone with Doug, and he's going to need you to move to the baby department for today. Molly is going home early."

"Okay," I said, not moving from beside the customer service desk. "I'll just get changed? And then go to the baby section?" I walked past the baby section almost every shift on the way to the break room. I didn't like the way it smelled. Plus, I'd never worked at the toy store as anything other than a cashier.

Pam looked at me with her eyebrows raised, then nodded her head sharply. "Good," she said.

I walked quickly to the back of the store. I tried to enter my employee code into the lock on the break room door. My hands kept slipping, and I accidentally hit two numbers at the same time. On my third try, the door opened.

The break room was a small room with hangers against one wall and lockers against another. A counter, fridge, microwave, and vending machine lined the back wall, and several tables were scattered in between. On the fourth wall was a whiteboard used to communicate important messages from management to the staff. It read:

> Notice! All sportswear sale items are to be scanned under the PLU/330 code until further notice. Hopefully all people will read this instead of asking stupid questions later.

Underneath that, someone else had written:

> doughnuts are for everyone. pls take <u>one</u> and have a Merry Christmas.

An empty box that had once contained doughnuts sat on the table nearest the whiteboard.

I turned away from the board and saw Molly standing by the lockers while Lisa helped her get her coat on. Molly's face was red and wet with tears. She breathed in a staccato rhythm until suddenly she heaved in a breath that seemed to get trapped in the upper part of her chest, not sinking in any further. Lisa was stroking the shoulder of Molly's puffy down coat. Molly reached up and wiped her eyes but continued to cry, flooding more tears down where the others had been.

"We'll wait in here for five more minutes," Lisa said to her. "Then Dave'll be here."

I had been introduced to Molly during my first shift over a month ago, but I hadn't seen much of her since. She was a stocky woman with short hair that curled tightly against her head. She had puffy eyes that made her look tired, although her skin looked soft. She usually managed the baby section but had been on a leave of absence recently. Apparently, she'd been pregnant this past year, but her baby had been stillborn. I didn't know too many details but had overheard Lisa screaming about it once, saying that the company was trying to force Molly back to work for the Christmas season, since the store was so busy.

"Can you imagine? Can you imagine coming back to this job? After all that?" She'd been yelling to someone, I can't remember who, but I remember them saying "shh," and then moving their hand as if they were pushing her words down towards the ground. She calmed down a little after that.

I stood and looked at Molly, and then she made eye contact with me. I put my head down and moved towards my locker. I opened the door and quickly pulled out my red vest with the always-attached nametag. I realized that I hadn't taken off my winter jacket yet, so I held my vest between my teeth while I struggled out of my coat. My arm got stuck in the sleeve, so I started shaking it hard. When I finally got my coat off, I jammed it into my locker and put on my vest. I was sweating a little underneath my armpits and down my back. Lisa and Molly moved towards the door of the break room, passing behind me. I thought that maybe I should turn around and say something, or turn around and smile, but I just stared really hard at the buttons on my vest as I did them up.

Once Molly and Lisa had left the break room, I gave them a couple of minutes and then exited myself. I went to the baby department, where Debbie and Connie were leaned up against the counter that held the computer for the baby shower registries. They were talking to each other and holding their hands up near their mouths and shaking their heads.

"Just awful," I heard one of them say.

One of them clicked her tongue against her teeth.

"Hi," I said as I approached them. "Pam said that Doug said that I should work in the baby department today."

Debbie and Connie barely glanced at me and then continued to talk to each other. I was sure they'd heard me.

"I've only worked cash before," I said, a little louder this time. Connie looked at me out of the corner of her eye. "Um, what do you want me to do?" I looked at Connie, and then she looked at Debbie.

"Okay," said Debbie. "Why don't you go tidy the feeding section?"

"Where is that?"

"Over there." She pointed to the back corner of the store at a sign that read Feeding Section.

I walked over to the section and saw a woman with her hands pushing against her lower back and her round belly sticking out in front of her. She looked incredibly pregnant. She had her coat under her arm and a plaid winter hat on her head. She held a card-board package that she was busy scrutinizing. I tried not to stare at her stomach.

She noticed me coming and looked me up and down. "Are these storage containers safe for the freezer?"

"Um," I said, leaning towards the product myself. "I don't know, but I'll ask."

"You don't know?"

"No, this is my first day." Then suddenly I felt a large hand spread against my left shoulder. Debbie was standing behind me.

"Can I help you with anything, ma'am?" she asked the woman.

"Yeah, I just want to know if these are safe for the freezer."

"Not those ones. We have others that are specifically for the freezer. I'll show you." Debbie turned to me. "Do you want to come along so you can see what to do?"

I didn't, but I nodded my head and fol-lowed them.

Debbie moved further down along the display. Everything in the feeding section was stacked in tidy rigid piles. The glossy packages all had pictures of brown-haired smiling women on them. Bright red letters that read Pump and Save stood out against yellow packaging. Debbie began pointing out the various types of breast milk storage containers available, and also the canvas zipper-bags to keep them in.

My eyes drifted to the different boxes on the shelf. There was a white plastic thing that looked like a couple of ice cube trays stacked on top of each other, which, I learned, was a baby bottle drying rack. More white-toothed women smiled out from packages containing bottles, topical breast cream, nipple shields, and nursing pads. This was all new to me. It occurred to me that there was a whole world of things out there that I didn't know about. There were so many things I hadn't thought of, didn't even know enough about to know that I hadn't thought of. I froze in one spot and moved my left hand to my breast. What the fuck did anyone need a nipple shield for?

"Did you get that?" Debbie turned and asked me as I quickly dropped my hand back down to my side. I saw the pregnant customer walking away from us.

"What? Oh, yeah," I said. Debbie shook

her head a little then went back to where Connie stood, near the computer.

I turned to my right and saw that the adjoining wall was filled with similar-looking boxes, all stacked neatly in perfect rows. The sign on the wall read Bath and Potty. Everything was in order, and I wasn't sure what there was for me to do. There were no holes in the display or gaps where new products needed to be added. I'd been avoiding the baby section until now, but clearly it was the cleanest section in the entire store.

I continued to scan the shelves until my eyes stopped on a prenatal heart listener. The box stood out to me because not only was there a picture of a woman on it, but a man stood just behind her with his arms around her. They both wore earphones and held a square piece of plastic over her large belly, his hand resting on top of hers. It was strange that I'd only noticed one picture of a couple so far.

It made me think, "It must be weird to be a guy," which was not the most brilliant thought I'd ever had. But then I realized that what I really meant was, Justin didn't even know that I was pregnant. He moved away so quickly, before I'd even had a chance to tell him. We were supposed to move to Whistler together, but he'd gone out first and met someone. Or maybe he knew her before he left. He changed his phone number and didn't leave a new one. Not that I really wanted to talk to him anyway, but I just couldn't imagine him walking around his shitty apartment, taking the lift up to the top of a ski hill, racing to get to work on time, kissing his new girlfriend on the lips, and all that time having no idea that he could be a father soon. I tried to imagine him with one pair of headphones and me with the other, listening to the heartbeat. The package said it only worked within the last months of pregnancy. I wasn't there yet.

I turned further to my right and looked at the small half-wall displaying about twelve different styles of baby shoes and some assorted baby bodysuits, apparently called "onesies." I'd heard that term for the first time years ago, when my cousin had used it at her baby shower.

"What's a onesie?" I'd asked.

"Kath," my cousin had said, "you are so never babysitting for me."

Over the top of the fake display wall I could see the blond hair of two women. They were browsing the items on the other side of the display.

"Oh my God! Oh my God, these are so cute."

"Oh my God! Your sister would so love this. It is so her."

"Ew, or look at this. I could get her chewable pregnancy heartburn tabs instead." She laughed and then pointed her finger down her throat, like she was going to gag herself. "Can you imagine?"

"I know, gawd."

"That is totally why I am never having kids."

"Exactly. I like your skirt."

"Thanks. It's new."

"But I totally know what I'm going to name my kids if I do have them."

"What?"

"Cassandra for a girl and Shaymis for a boy."

"Shaymis? Oh my God, that is so cool. Did you make that up?"

"Yeah, and I would spell it with a 'y.'"

"Oh my God, awesome. Like, so how much *is* this?"

"Yeah, so why aren't there any prices on anything here?"

I opened my eyes wide and took a deep breath in. I looked over to the computer. Connie had gone, but Debbie still stood there. She had noticed the two women and was flicking her hand towards them while looking at me. I figured that I had almost seven hours left in my shift. I moved around to the other side of the small display and stood next to the two young women.

"Can I help you?" I asked, and smiled.

The first girl turned to me and then elbowed her friend. The second girl turned and looked at me too, frowning.

"No," she said. "We're fine."

And then my stomach tensed up. I felt like the skin under my chin was sagging and like there was too much saliva at the back of my throat. I put one hand on my stomach, and with the other, I reached out to the fake display wall for support.

"Ew," said one of the girls. "What is she doing?"

Suddenly, I gagged. I couldn't control myself. Red and yellow vomit hit the floor in front of the two girls. Some of it splashed up onto one girl's shoes. Her new skirt was spared.

"Oh my God," she hollered.

Debbie ran over and looked at the two girls.

"I'm so sorry," she said. I felt her hand on my back. "You need to go to the washroom," she said. "You should go sit down."

I held on to Debbie and tried to steady myself against her. I remembered that when I was little, I used to cry every time I puked. My mom would give me flat ginger ale and tell me that she'd done the same thing when she was younger.

Debbie helped me to the washroom. I sat on the edge of the toilet seat and held my head in my hands. I didn't want to cry at work, so I kept taking deep breaths, but it was no use. I needed someone to explain what was happening to me. I wanted to know it could be okay, that I could be happy with a baby, like the women in the ads. Or I wanted to go back to not knowing, like those sorority girls with their fucking skirt and their avant-garde spelling. I slammed my closed fist against my forehead. How many people did this alone, really?

I stood up and looked in the mirror. I looked into my own dark swollen eyes. If I could focus on something besides the crying, then I would stop. I had seven hours left in my shift.

Sam

Elizabeth had decided that she wasn't going home for Christmas, because she was tired of her family—her sister's drama, her brother's selfishness, and her mother's criticisms—but when the time finally came, she found that she couldn't stop thinking of Sam. Her stepdad had always loved Christmas, and Elizabeth knew that this one could be his last. She thought about him often. She missed him. After weeks of repeatedly telling her friends and neighbours that she was looking forward to spending the holiday alone, Elizabeth finally decided to fly home on Christmas Eve.

She took a cab from the airport, then stood in the driveway outside of her family's home.

The street around the house was cold and empty, and the shrubs in front of the bare porch were wrapped in brown burlap. But the windows were foggy with moisture from body heat, and she could hear the low thump of music and laughter. She walked up the driveway.

When she got to the front door, it flew open. The interior of the house was blinding, throbbing with the glow of red and white Christmas lights. Three of Elizabeth's older cousins, all with cigarettes stuck in their lips and drinks in their hands, pushed out onto the porch.

"Hey," said Eliot as he stepped outside. "I heard you weren't coming."

"Well," she said, "I guess I changed my mind." Eliot was carrying two beers in his left hand and removed the cigarette from his mouth with the other.

"You've got your work cut out for you," Elizabeth said, nodding towards his full hands.

"Yeah, Charlotte is pregnant again, so I'm drinking for two now."

"Congrats."

He grinned.

Inside the house, the main room was full of people, all relatives on Elizabeth's mother's side. Four uncles gathered around the buffet, filling their round bellies with ginger cookies decorated to look like Santa Claus.

Elizabeth put down her duffel bag and took off her boots. There was such a bustle inside that no one seemed to notice her arrival, even as she continued down the hallway and into the kitchen. The house smelled like scented candles, and a rock 'n' roll Christmas album played behind the din. Elizabeth's mother was standing at the kitchen counter, pouring vodka into a jigger.

"You've *got* to try a candy-cane martini," she said to Elizabeth's aunt Louise, who stood next to her mother, holding a full glass of wine in her hand.

"That sounds neat," said Louise. She swayed a little as she spoke.

Elizabeth took off her coat and hung it on the back of a kitchen chair.

Elizabeth's mother turned around, and their eyes met as she continued shaking the jigger.

"You can put that in the closet, please,"

she said.

Elizabeth moved back down the hallway without saying a word. The hallway closet was full of coats, and there didn't seem to be any extra hangers, so she threw her coat on the floor, on top of all the boots. Elizabeth fantasized about the candy-cane martini.

She moved back towards the kitchen. This time, her mother met her halfway, in the middle of the hallway. Her mother reached out and grabbed Elizabeth by both shoulders and threw her into her chest, into a strong hug.

"You look good," she said, releasing Elizabeth from the hug but still holding her shoulders. "You look healthy."

"Healthy?" Elizabeth frowned. "What does that mean?"

"I don't know. You were too thin before."

"I've put on weight?"

"No, I didn't mean that. It's just that you usually have dark circles under your eyes, but now you don't. Are you still off the—"

"Yes."

They stared at each other for a moment, trapped in the narrow hallway, each one blocking the other from moving.

"Where's Sam?" Elizabeth finally asked.

"In the living room."

Elizabeth walked through the crowd of people towards the living room. She was interrupted by her sister, who appeared from out of the crowd, holding a glass of red wine and smiling.

"Hey, Liz," she said.

"Hi, Brittany." Elizabeth stared at her wine glass for a second, then looked her sister up and down. Brittany wore a slim-fitting black dress with a crew neck, as well as sheer tights and a pair of kitten heels that matched both her lipstick and nail polish. Her hair was freshly dyed and delicately curled around her face. She wore dark heavy eye makeup that made her look old, but otherwise, she looked pretty and stylish. Elizabeth folded her arms across her chest. "I'm so sorry about you and John," she said.

Brittany shrugged. "Maybe it was the best thing that could have happened to me." She shrugged again. In fact, it seemed that she had started shrugging and couldn't stop. "I know. Who ever thought that *I* would get jilted?" She laughed and took a drink of wine. "I had to return all the gifts, send out notices of cancellation, and we didn't take out insurance on the honeymoon. But you know what?" She looked at Elizabeth. "Who. Cares. I'm better off without him." She took another big drink from her glass.

"Why not go on the honeymoon anyway? Take a friend. Just to get away."

"I never really wanted to go to Cuba," she said, still shrugging. "I wanted to go to Paris." Brittany sipped her wine, then she looked at Elizabeth as though she were suddenly embarrassed. "Oh, Lizzy, I'm so sorry."

"For what?"

"Does this bother you?" She glanced at her wine glass.

"No." It was Elizabeth's turn to shrug.

She smiled. "Well, I should have known, I guess, when I said Paris and he said Cuba, that things weren't right between us."

"How's Mom taking it?" Elizabeth's mother was desperate for one of her kids to have a wedding. She said she'd always known that Brittany would be the first.

"She wants us to try and work it out." Brittany pointed at the ceiling with her free hand. "Not. Happening."

"Is Carl here?"

"No," Brittany said, her curls bouncing as she shook her head. "He stayed in Calgary. He makes double time if he works on a holiday. Plus, he's spending time with his lady, I guess." Brittany rolled her eyes and took another drink.

"You've met her?" Their brother Carl moved to Alberta three years ago and had only made one trip home since then. His life out there was mysterious to the rest of the family.

"No, but I've seen some photos." Brittany moved towards Elizabeth and whispered. "Total. Skank." She stepped away again. "Just like Carl to end up with some tart."

"Maybe she's nice."

"Hmm. Doubtful. You can tell a lot about a book just by its cover," Brittany insisted. Then she looked at Elizabeth's jeans and striped dress shirt. Elizabeth was standing in her socked feet and shifting her weight uncomfortably.

"It's been a long few months, hasn't it?" Elizabeth finally said, trying to smile.

"Hell. Yes."

"Have you seen Sam?"

Brittany looked down. "It's not good, Lizzy. You know," she said, shaking her head. "Everyone has one parent that they really don't want to see go *first*."

Elizabeth paused, then said, "I wanted to come see him."

Brittany nodded. "It's good that you did. He's in the living room." She looked back over her left shoulder at the buffet. "I'll catch you soon." Brittany nodded slowly as she turned to walk away.

When Elizabeth turned to face the living room, she saw Sam sitting alone in a sofa chair. He was a short man and looked tiny in the oversized furniture. Elizabeth wanted to check to see if his feet touched the ground.

There was a time when Sam's neck was barely distinguishable from his shoulders. They had joined in one tense group of muscle and vein. He and Elizabeth used to have a game they'd play together when she was small, a show they liked to perform in front of others. He'd grab onto the hair at the top of her head and pretend to lift her up that way. She would actually be holding onto his wrists, but she'd scream as though she were in horrible pain. Now, at fifty-nine, the skin hung loose around Sam's neck. He'd lost a lot of weight in the last year, since starting radiation treatment. He could barely lift his drink up off the coffee table and bring it to his mouth.

"You made it," Sam said when Elizabeth came into the room. "Here." He struggled to pull the ottoman out from beside his chair. "I saved you a seat."

"How are things?" She asked him, moving the ottoman herself and sitting down.

"Oh, you know." Sam smiled. His eyes were icy blue. Elizabeth had been ten years old when Sam married her mom. Carl was eight, and Brittany was five. Sam had always been an intensely private man, so even his stepkids knew little about him. He'd moved to Ontario from Nova Scotia as a young man, and he sometimes talked about missing the ocean. But then he'd get quiet again, and his blue eyes would look away, somewhere else.

Sam and Elizabeth sat on the periphery of the get-together, turned so that they were both facing the crowd of people. Sam offered her a drink, but she declined.

"We've got pop, too," he assured her. "And juice."

"Nothing right now," she said.

"How's that going?" he asked, glancing towards his own light beer.

"Still fine," she said. "One hundred and twenty-six days."

"One day at a time, isn't that what they say?"

"Sure is."

"I'm proud of you," he said. Elizabeth looked away from Sam, taking in the room around her. Her mother had decorated the tree this year using only tinsel and white Christmas lights. A family of stuffed reindeer sat in the middle of the coffee table. There were three poinsettias visible from where Elizabeth sat.

"Your mother did a nice job this year," Sam said.

"Hm." Elizabeth nodded.

"She loves you very much," he said, touching her knee with his hand. When Elizabeth turned slightly, he took his hand back.

"I'm so thirsty," Elizabeth thought, but

she couldn't stand the idea of going back into the kitchen.

"I noticed that Buffalo to San Francisco is only a hundred and twenty-nine dollars return," Sam said.

"You thinking of going?"

"I don't think so," he said. "You should go. You'd like San Francisco."

"Yeah, but I don't think I'll be able to get away from work any time soon."

An explosion of laughter came from the kitchen. One uncle's voice boomed above the rest. It was followed by shrill squeals from some of the aunts and female cousins. John Cougar Mellencamp's version of "I Saw Mommy Kissing Santa Claus" started playing on the stereo.

"I used to love Christmas," Sam said.

"Yeah, me too."

Sam turned to look out the window beside him. The skin on the back of his neck was as white as the snow outside. He turned back to Elizabeth.

"Remember that one Christmas, when we made that snowman to hang in the window?" he asked.

"Of course. That was so long ago."

Sam took a sip of his beer. His hand shook as he brought the heavy glass to his lips.

"You must have been about eleven or twelve," he said. "I remember I used to get so excited for Christmas morning when you kids were little.

"You were just on the verge of being too old for Santa." He looked towards the ceiling as the memory came to him. "You were asking questions like, 'All the houses? In the *whole* world? In *one* night?'" He chuckled. "I wanted you to stay a kid for a while longer. I wasn't going to burst your bubble." Sam started to cough. He picked up a napkin near him and held it to his mouth. He coughed hard for several seconds, then relaxed again. He looked at Elizabeth and shook his head, then leaned back and closed his eyes.

Elizabeth swung the ottoman to the other side of Sam's chair, sitting with her back to the room, closing off her and Sam from the crowd around them. She didn't want to be this close to Sam's illness, it was too unbearable, but she couldn't leave. Elizabeth wanted to change the subject. She spoke quickly, not making eye contact with Sam. "Brittany says that Carl's new lady is a tart, but she's just upset about John, and she'll never be happy for anyone else. She's always been like that. But who gets engaged to someone they've only known for three months?" Compared to Sam's degenerating health, family gossip felt constant and reliable.

"You are surrounded by good people," Sam said, still resting his head against the back of the chair. He looked at Elizabeth. "We all have our problems, our flaws. All of us."

Elizabeth shook her head. She had tears in her eyes.

"I don't fit in here," she said.

"You're good people too, Elizabeth," he said.

"How come I only hear about my mistakes? How come Mom only tells me what I'm doing wrong?"

"She worries. She isn't perfect."

"And Carl can't stand us, that's clear." Elizabeth looked up at Sam, meeting his eyes at last.

"Leaving is the right thing to do sometimes," he said. "But when you want to stay and can't. Well...."

Sam closed his eyes. His face was pale. The room was hot. His chest moved as he breathed. His mouth was open slightly. Conversations grew louder in the crowded house. There were vanilla-scented candles burning nearby. Elizabeth opened her mouth to speak, to tell Sam not to go. She didn't have the words in her mind yet, but she had to speak anyway. "I want a drink," she said, "so bad. I'm not strong enough—"

"Elizabeth." Sam sat forward and their eyes met again. "How many times do you think we live?"

Elizabeth stared at him.

"Because you know what I think?" he said. "I think that once is enough."

Elizabeth pressed her chin into her neck, tilting her head forward so that her tears fell onto her lap. "What are we all going to do?" she asked.

Sam leaned back in his chair. "We are going to enjoy Christmas together." He took a sip of his beer. "Your mother did a wonderful job." He smiled. Elizabeth touched his knee. She would have sat there all night. She would have stayed there for days, for weeks, forever, on the periphery of the Christmas cheer, sitting next to Sam.

Red Earrings

My alarm clock went off at ten a.m., and I let it ring while I began to turn my head slowly from side to side. My small bed had two thin pillows that hurt my neck, and every morning I swore I would replace them soon, but I never seemed to get around to it. I had to get my day started, but, as usual, I was not looking forward to work. Despite the discomfort of my little bed, all I wanted was to stay there all day. This would be my fourteenth workday in a row, but I knew that tomorrow was my day off, and I used that thought to pull myself awake.

It had been two months since I'd moved back in with my parents. I'd recently acquired a small dresser from one of my aunts, and this added a sense of organization to my life. I sat on the edge of my bed and leaned over towards the dresser. I searched one of the drawers for my work clothes. I found my white dress shirt and a cleanish pair of jeans.

I went to the bathroom and quickly brushed my teeth. I didn't floss. When I put my toothbrush away, I noticed an old pair of earrings at the back of the drawer. They were red, dangling, prohibited by the dress code at work, and I was running late. But I decided to put them on. I threaded the hooks through my earlobes, then I looked at myself in the mirror. When I'd moved away to go to art school, I hadn't taken these earrings with me, even though they'd been my favourite accessory at the time. I'd nearly forgotten about them.

I went downstairs and poured myself a bowl of cereal. My mom was sitting at the kitchen table in her Molly Maid uniform, reading the paper and having a coffee and a cigarette. It seemed I wasn't the only one on the afternoon shift that day.

My mom was shaking her head. "I cannot believe those idiots gave Bush another term."

"I know. Me neither."

"Sounds like his win's being contested again." She shook her head some more. "Crooks! All of them!" She was shouting. Then she looked up at me.

"Are those new earrings?" she asked.

"No, I just forgot that I had them."

"They look lovely on you. You should wear them every day."

My face got hot. I was not used to her being so nice, especially so early in the day.

"Thanks," I said, keeping my eyes on my cereal bowl. "But I'm just going to have to take them off when I get to work."

"How come?"

"Flashy jewellery is against dress code."

"So tell them where to shove it."

"I don't—"

"Seriously, Kathleen. You need to stand up for yourself more."

"I guess."

"Those asshole bosses need to be put in their place once in a while."

I finished my cereal and put the bowl in the sink.

"Rinse it!" my mom yelled. I rinsed it.

"Whatever. Tomorrow's my day off. I've

worked every day for the past two weeks."

"Those bastards'd make you work Christmas day if it wasn't illegal. Sheesh."

"Think I can get a ride to work?" I asked.

My mom looked at her watch. "You should get up a little earlier if you need a ride."

"I don't *need* a ride. I was just asking."

She pursed her lips, staring at me as she butted out her cigarette. "I guess it doesn't matter if I'm a little late for work," she said.

"If it's going to make you late, then never mind. I was just asking."

"No, no," she said, picking up her purse and tossing it, somewhat aggressively, over her shoulder. "Get in the car. I'll drive you."

"Mom, if you don't have time—"

"I have time. Just get up a little earlier next time you need a ride." She thudded down the front hallway and out the front door. As soon as she was on the porch, she stuck her head back inside. "But I'm leaving *right now.*"

I slipped my feet into my winter boots and walked to the car with my laces undone.

Inside the break room at work, I got into my red vest with my already-attached nametag. KATHLEEN was written in crayon font next to the Toys-O-Rama logo. I was still wearing the dangling red earrings. I thought about what my mom said, about standing up for myself, so I told myself that I didn't give a shit about the dress code. And what difference did it make anyway? And, hey, at least they matched my uniform. And if every other one of my co-workers could have a perm, then I could at least wear a pair of dangling earrings. But I took them off before I closed my locker and shoved them into my coat pocket.

"Hi, Pam," I said as I approached the customer service desk.

"Back from your break?"

"No, I just got here now."

"Oh," she shook her head. "I thought I saw you before."

"You're probably thinking of yesterday."

She looked at her watch. "What time does your shift start?"

"At eleven."

"Sure it's not ten forty-five?"

"No, it says eleven on the schedule."

"Well, it isn't a bad idea to be here fifteen minutes early anyway. You can take register five."

I went to the register and punched in my employee number and password. Then I felt a hand on my right arm.

"Kathleen." I looked across to see Debbie leaned over from the register beside mine. "Did Pam tell you about the counterfeit bills?"

"No," I said.

"The store has been getting lots of fake bills lately." Debbie looked over her right shoulder, then her left, and then faced me, still holding onto my arm. "Six hundred dollars," she mouthed with extreme intensity but barely any sound.

"Whoa," I said.

"Make sure you check all the bills. Doug said that if anyone takes a counterfeit bill, it may have to come out of their paycheque."

"How are we supposed to check them?"

"You rub them against a piece of paper."

"That's it?"

"Yes. Real bills will leave a mark because they have a special ink that never dries."

"A special ink?" I said.

Debbie nodded vigorously with her eyes wide.

"Yup," she said.

"Are you opened?" a customer asked, her arms full of dinky cars. She plunked her purchase down at my till. She was a heavy woman with wavy blond hair and cakey face makeup. She was wearing a light grey golf shirt with neon green writing that read Ontario Biotechnologists Conference 1998.

"Can you double-bag it for me? I got a long walk to the car."

When I finished with the customer, Carly, my co-worker, arrived at the register immediately behind my own and began to get set up for her shift. Carly was a skinny red-headed single mother. At age twenty-four she was wise beyond her years. She was quietly singing the chorus to Ol' Dirty Bastard's "Got Your Money."

She looked up at me, shaking her head gently. "I still can't believe he's gone. Dirty had another great album in him." She moved her hands to her hips and looked up to the ceiling, as if searching for answers. "What a motherfucking tragedy." Then she logged into her till. "Fuck!" Carly's head whipped forward, and our eyes met. "Did you hear about this counterfeit bill shit? They said if we take a counterfeit bill, it's coming out of our pay. Like, what the fuck, eh?"

A woman pushed her loaded shopping cart up to Carly's register. Carly turned and smiled.

"Hi there. Find everything okay today?"

I turned away from Carly and faced the store.

Then there came an odd moment of misplaced serenity when there were no customers at the cash registers, though I could see that the store was brimming with shoppers. I stood at my till with my arms crossed. I thought about the red dangling earrings in my coat pocket. I imagined them drooping from my ears, with my hair swept up off my shoulders and the earrings showing off a feminine curve in my neck. I thought of how I might look to someone else, coming through the line. How they might see me and think, "That is the prettiest cashier I have ever seen." But I realized that the earrings would match my red vest with the embroidered zebra on the back and the ever-pinned nametag and would only accentuate my uniform.

The phone at my till rang.

"Kathleen speaking," I said into the receiver.

"Dude, you look so fucking bored." It was Carly.

"Guess why."

"If Wanda sees you, she'll fucking freak."

"There is nothing to do. If I have no customers, I have nothing to do."

"Well, she'll find you something to do, and then she'll find me something to do too. You've got to *look* like you're busy, at least."

"How?"

"Pretend like you're looking for something on the floor around your till."

"If there is nothing for me to do, then they should just send me home."

"Good fucking luck. I had a toothache so bad yesterday I thought I was going to fucking shoot myself. You think Doug would let me leave five minutes early?"

"Doug's a dick."

"Like I don't fucking know that. And tomorrow I told them I want the day off to take my kid to see Santa, and they said only if I find someone to work for me. So what the fuck? Then my kid doesn't get to see Santa?"

I turned and looked at Carly. Her red hair was pulled back in a ponytail, and her hand that wasn't holding the phone was waving angrily at her side. I wasn't scheduled to work tomorrow.

"It must be so cool to still believe in Santa," I said, moving the subject away from shift coverage.

"Yeah, so cool. A big fucking lineup and then ten bucks for a photo." Carly's scrunched-up forehead quickly relaxed. "You have a customer," she said and then hung up the phone.

My customer was a twentysomething man with a backwards baseball cap and a few thin wisps of dark hair lying across his upper lip. He was buying a three-dollar jigsaw puzzle with a picture of Ginger Spice on it. It was from the clearance section.

"Hi there. Did you find everything you were looking for today?"

He grunted without making eye contact.

"Okay, so that's three forty-five," I said.

He pulled out a fifty-dollar bill. I took it from his hand and looked at it. The bill felt thinner than it should have been, and Mackenzie King looked ill.

"So, from fifty?" I said looking at him.

"Mm-hmm," he said.

"No problem. But just to let you know, we're checking all large bills." I pulled some paper out of the receipt printer and wiped the bill on it. There was no mark.

The boy began to squirm.

"I just need to give my manager a call," I said. "It'll only take a minute."

"Yo, it's cool, it's cool." He plunged his hands down to his sides and began shifting his weight back and forth.

"It's no trouble," I said, picking up the receiver of the phone at my till. I hit the page button and then said, "Manager on duty to register five please. Manager to register five."

"I'll just, uh...yo, don't worry. I, uh...I have other money in my car. I'll just go and get it." He ran out of the store.

Derrick came to my till and gave me a warm smile.

"Hey, Kath. What's the problem?"

Derrick was young and handsome with jeans that sat on his hips and hair that always looked like he'd just rolled out of bed.

"Someone tried to pay with this fifty, but when I called you to come check it, he ran out of the store."

"No way," Derrick said, examining the bill. "Nice job, Kath. This is totally fake, and you did the right thing by calling me." He gave me a thumbs up and smiled again. "You've really caught on fast around here."

I blushed and turned back to face my till. "Thanks, Derrick."

Pam came over to where we stood. "Is everything okay?"

"It's fine," Derrick said. "Kathleen just made a really good call on a customer who was trying to use a counterfeit bill. She's doing a great job."

"Well," Pam said, "good to hear." She headed back to the customer service desk.

I was in a good mood for the rest of my shift.

Once my shift was over, I went back to the break room. I got into my winter coat and put on the red earrings. I made sure to say goodbye to Derrick before I left.

"Have a great night," he said, waving and giving me a wink.

It was cold outside, but I didn't feel like calling home to ask for a ride, so I decided to walk. I crossed the cold parking lot and then took the bridge over the highway. The wind was ferocious, and without a hat on, the frozen metal earrings whipped against my face and tugged at my numb ear lobes. I took them off and put them back in my pocket.

After the bridge, the sidewalk narrowed and then disappeared. I walked through a dirt path rimmed by sparse grass and weeds on both sides. I remembered when this area had been farmers' fields. Yellow cow corn had come up to my eyeballs. I used to think that my family could go out there together, pick our own food, take it back home, and cook it on our gas-powered stove.

You couldn't eat that corn, my dad said. It was just for cows.

I never saw a cow.

I peered into the dark spaces between the houses. I thought I saw something glimmer, like a small pair of eyes reflecting some distant ambient light. I got scared, and as I quickened my pace, I tried to imagine Easter eggs hidden there, put there years ago and left where no one had found them, their shiny wrappers barely hidden, or barely exposed. But in my head, they became moldy and melting, like foil-covered corpses, dumped. I shuddered and began to run along the frozen path.

I was nearly out of breath when I arrived at my parents' house. Inside, my mom and dad were sitting on the couch. Dad was in his pajamas, but Mom still had her work uniform on. She must have just gotten home. They were watching television. They both wore reading glasses bought from Shoppers Drug Mart and sat frowning at the blue glow of their enormous TV set. I stood in the doorway, struggling with my winter boots. My mom looked up at me from where she sat.

"No hat!" she exclaimed.

"I forgot it."

"You should have called for a ride."

"I like walking though."

"Well, then you should have brought your hat."

I took off my boots while canned laughter exploded out of the TV set. My mom got up and moved into the kitchen, walking as though her left leg had fallen asleep.

"There is leftover chicken in the fridge," she said.

"I'm not really hungry. Dad, can you turn that down for a second?"

"Why?" he yelled. "I can't hear it with you two yelling."

"I don't think we're yelling," I said.

"You've got to eat something," my mom said from the kitchen.

"I'd rather just have tea, something warm."

"How about I make you a roast beef sandwich?" she asked.

My dad turned the volume louder in the living room. A thump came from the kitchen, like an entire cow had been dropped on the counter. I remained in the front entrance. Before I took off my winter coat, I stuck my hands in the pockets and felt the red earrings. I held them in my hand as I took off my scarf.

Without answering my mom, I went to the upstairs bathroom. I warmed my hands under the tap and then rubbed the feeling back into my ears. I put the earrings on and then went downstairs.

My mom was sitting on the couch again.

"If you just want tea, it's in the cupboard," she said.

Dad turned up the volume further.

"Dad, the television is really loud."

"I guess since it's my house, I figured I could listen to the TV as loud as I want," he replied.

I put the kettle on to boil and then sat with my parents in the living room. They were watching *Jeopardy!* As Alex Trebek was about to begin getting to know the contestants, my mom turned to me.

"So, you got away with the earrings?" she asked.

I nodded.

She playfully hit my dad on the arm. "Turn it down. Your daughter's had a long day at work," she said.

My dad turned the TV down.

"Lots of brats to deal with?" he asked me.

"It's not the brats that are the problem, it's the managers. But they were nice to me today. I stopped a guy from paying with a fake fifty."

"Do you get a bonus for that?" my dad asked.

"Yeah," my mom snorted, "they gave her the fake fifty."

"No, they just told me I'm doing a good job." I looked at my mom. "They told me that I'm really fitting in around the store."

"Oh yeah," my mom said, rolling her eyes. "Those jerks love to butter you up so they can take advantage of you later. I know *all* about it."

We stared at the television as the Double Jeopardy! round started.

"Is Ken Jennings still winning?" I said.

"Sure is," my dad said. He loved Ken Jennings, who had so far won more consecutive *Jeopardy!* episodes than any other contestant in the history of the show.

"I think it's fixed," my mom said.

"He's, what, a bartender or something in real life?" I asked.

"Is that right?" my mom asked. "Just a

working stiff."

"I should try and go on *Jeopardy!*," I said.

My dad stared at the TV, and my mom made a nervous humming noise.

"What?" I asked.

"You want to go on *Jeopardy!*?" my mom said.

"Why not apply for a painting job?" my dad said.

"Like, you mean painting houses?" I asked.

"No. Pictures."

"What kind of job do you think exists that is called 'painting pictures'?"

"Maybe you should have asked yourself that question before you went to art school," he said. My mom hit him on the arm again.

"I know," I said. "I should go back in time and make a different decision."

"Yeah," my dad chuckled. "If only." He lit a cigarette.

The kettle began to whistle. I went to the kitchen and shut off the burner.

"I'm going to my room," I said.

"You don't want to sit with us?" my mom asked.

"I feel tired. I'm going to lie down."

"You sleep too much," my mom said.

I turned towards the staircase. "I think I'm going to go to work tomorrow," I said.

"What?" my mom asked. "I thought it was your one day off?"

"Well, my friend needs someone to cover for her."

My mother snorted disapprovingly. "I told you, Kath, that if you don't stand up for yourself, they'll take advantage," she said and turned back to the TV.

I walked up the stairs and then stopped on the landing. I thought about Carly and her son. I could easily take her shift tomorrow. I should have offered earlier. I imagined how happy Carly would be when I called her with the news. Plus, I figured Derrick would be at work tomorrow too, and I was a little surprised at how much I wanted to see him again.

I went into my parents' room to use the phone. I called the store and got Carly's number, then I called her at home.

"Hello." Carly sounded glum on the phone, and I wondered if it was ODB related.

"Carly? It's Kathleen."

"Kath!" she said.

"Find anyone to take your shift for tomorrow?"

"Fuck yes! Stacy from the video game department's going to do it. She's so fucking balls out!"

"Oh," I said. "Well, okay. Great."

We said goodbye, and I hung up the phone. I walked back to the hallway and thought about returning to the living room. I looked at my parents, who were silently watching the loud TV. The blue light from the screen flickered against their bodies. I shivered, still feeling cold from the walk home.

Acknowledgements

Mikhail Iossel was instrumental in helping develop this collection in its earliest stages. Marcie Frank was an especially insightful reader. Thanks to everyone in the Concordia University creative writing program who read and gave feedback on early versions of these stories. Special thanks to Kasia Juno and Katrina Best for their amazing support as writers and friends. Cheers to Katrina for coming up with the title *Entry Level*.

Very special thanks to Jon Paul Fiorentino for doing a wonderful job editing the book and designing the cover.

Sincere thanks to everyone at Insomniac.

I am grateful to my family for their continued support and to Sean Springer for his love and encouragement. Thanks to Jayne Hildebrand for being so cool.

An earlier version of "The Baby Section" originally appeared in *Matrix* magazine.

Many of these stories were developed and workshopped throughout the course of my master's degree, which was generously funded by SSHRC and the FQRSC. I am also deeply indebted to Terry Byrnes, who did a brilliant job supervising my thesis, in which many of these stories appeared.